Domestic Courage

By
Perry Comer

ISBN: 9781077085541

In Memory
of

Freddie Comer

BOOKS BY PERRY COMER

The Prize
(Donland)

The Messenger
Donland and the Hornet

Donland's Ransom
Donland and the Hornet

Raid on Port Royal
Donland and the Hornet

The Bond of Duty
Donland and the Hornet

Seige
Donland and The Hornet

The Rescue
Donland and the Hornet

The Snake Killer
(Juvenile Action/adventure)

God's Broken Man
(Allan Brooks) (Christian Fiction)

Myrtle Beach Murder
(Allan Brooks)(Christian Fiction)

Fall of Fort Fisher
(Juvenile action/adventure)
(Civil War)

Andrew's War
(Juvenile action/adventure)
(Civil War)

Fighting Marines: Hardy's Commission

Fighting Marines: Hardy's Challenge

Chapter One

Hornet sat with her sails furled and lashed. She tugged lightly at her anchors while riding the small rollers. Donland smiled as he likened English Harbor to a Connecticut lake on a hot lazy August afternoon. The lush green hills on the other side of the harbor reminded him of the peaceful countryside he had walked when he was just a boy. It was so long ago that the memories were hazy and dream-like. So too were his memories of the trapper who had rescued him and his brother from the well where his father had hid them before the Indians attacked. His mind drifted to the chandler's shop in which he had been apprenticed. What was vivid in his mind was the he was plucked from the chandler's shop to begin a new life afloat, one that carried forward to this day.

The future concerned him more than the past. The war was over, *Hornet* may tug at her anchors yearning to be free but she like him remained tethered to the land and to the decisions others were to make about both. Her fate would decide his. The Admiralty in London was decommissioning its aging fleet and in the process casting hundreds of serving officers onto the beach. The naval assets in the West Indies were being pared and officers of note and peerage were shifted to other ships or recalled to London. Admiral Pigot's seventy-four-gun ship, *Warrior*, lay at anchor reminding all in Antigua that the world as it had been was changed.

Nine whole weeks had come and gone since dropping the hook. *Stinger* lay two hundred yards away, her sails stored and her guns removed with only watch keepers remaining. She was to be sold. Her captain, Powell, was reduced in rank back to lieutenant and was ashore waiting his final disposition. Before leaving his beloved *Stinger* he had stood on *Hornet*'s deck and wistfully said while staring across at *Stinger*, "I'll not have the opportunity again." Donland had said nothing to the remark for he knew the same fate awaited him. He had neither peerage nor a person of privilege that could speak on his behalf.

"Captain, Sir," Bill intruded into Donland's gloomy thoughts.

"Yes, Bill?" Donland responded.

"Boat be comin, see thar," Bill said and pointed.

Bill and his mates had surprised him by choosing to stay aboard even after being told they would no longer be paid. "We've no home but *Hornet*!" Bill had said while speaking for the twenty-three freed slaves Donland had taken off a slaver some years earlier. "We stay for free and food," the proud man had stated. So Donland fed them from his own pursue as he was doing for David, Simon and Honest. Those remaining aboard were a quarter of the ship's complement and no officers remained.

The boat was making for *Hornet*. Donland pulled a glass from the rack and focused on the figure sitting in the stern. He was mildly surprised to see Sumerford but glad. It was at times such as this that a man needed a friend. He hoped Sumerford bore a letter from Betty, he'd not heard from her in over six months.

"Duced hot is it not?" Sumerford said as he gained the deck.

"Aye," Donland answered as he clasped his friend's hand.

"Let's go below, I've a cool bottle of claret."

"Water will be preferable. I'd my fill of wine last evening with the governor and Admiral Pigot. A wasted evening, I might add."

"I would hazard that you as I, am unemployed or soon to be."

Sumerford only smiled.

"I take your smile to be a no and that you are here in some government capacity," Donland stated.

Sumerford again said nothing as they descended the hatch.

As they entered the cabin, Honest set a clay pitcher of water on the recently cleared table.

"I'm delighted you have companionship during your incarceration," Sumerford said upon seeing Honest.

"Aye, and I'd ask for none better," Donland answered.

Honest poured water into two glasses. He said while pouring water for Sumerford, "The devil's misplaced one of his own, else you'd not be here."

"I take that to mean that you are delighted to have me aboard," Sumerford said taking the glass.

Honest smiled broadly and added, "The time here has not been without it's comforts but you coming aboard is not to my liking. In past days, you've brought more than one misery and seeing you is not only a reminder of such but also a warning of more to come. I'd wager a month's pay, were I being paid a month's wage, that you've some scheme that will cost a poor sailor blood."

Donland sensed needless words were about to spoken, he asked, "Have you news of Betty?"

Sumerford winked at Honest and answered, "A letter, a rather thick one resides right here." He then tapped his breast pocket. "You'll have it after we have talked a bit. I'd not want your mind wandering to words you've only half read in your haste to devour her letter."

Donland's face flushed with anger but he managed to forestall it and let it pass. Sumerford was toying with him and it did not set well. "By gawd, then get on with it man!"

Sumerford did not smile but rather drank again from the glass. He produced a handkerchief from his sleeve and patted his lips then sat.

David tapped at the doorpost, "Sir, may I join?" he asked.

"Aye, you may as well for I'm of the mind that this will concern you," Donland said.

Sumerford faced the boy, "Yes, it concerns you so you may as well be a party to it. And, lest I forget, I've a letter for you." He reached into his other breast pocket and pulled out a small white envelope and handed in David's direction.

"A letter?" The boy said with surprise as he stepped forward for the envelope. "I don't know anyone who would write."

David examined the envelope and his face burst into a broad smile, "It's from Betty Sumerford!"

Donland was not amused. "Get on with it!" he blurted.

"Sit and I will tell you why I've come," Sumerford said harshly.

Donland pulled a chair from the table and sat. David looked from the envelope to Donland and then to Sumerford. He stuffed the envelope into his pocket.

Sumerford faced Donland and said, "I'm here to negotiate the purchase of two surplus vessels the sloop *Hornet* and the sloop *Stinger.*"

Donland stared dumbfounded at Sumerford.

Sumerford held up his hand as if to say, "Say nothing I've more to add."

He began, "You indicated that you were curious about my employment status, I am here to buy vessels for the new navy."

"Which navy is that?" Donland asked.

"The United States, your recent adversary."

"And yours," Donland added.

"Yes, it was as you said but no longer. I have made my amends and am assisting in the purchase of vessels to be fitted out as men of war. As you know, I have business concerns from Charleston to Boston and as a resident of both cities I am as much a one of them as any man. It was therefore only logical that I should offer my services to my homeland."

"And those services are to purchase warships from the crown for pennies and to receive hefty commissions for doing so?" Donland asked.

"Business, Isaac, just plain old-fashioned commerce," Sumerford said and lifted the glass to drink. He swallowed and continued, "The Admiralty intends to sell off all foreign built small vessels. Their larger older vessels will either be broken up or sunk, as these are no longer needed. The snobs intend a British only navy and that holds true for officers. Those not born on English soil will be sent home with a shilling or two and nothing more." He paused to allow Donland to digest the words. Seeing in Donland's eyes the realization of his words he said, "Once the sale is completed, and it will be so I was assured last night, you will be unemployed and with few prospects. I'm sure you have given thought to your future have you not?"

Donland nodded. He chose his words with care. "I dared hope for orders but after the first month at anchor and the orders those in similar circumstances as mine received, I lost hope of such. As to my future, once I've received my papers, I shall endeavor to purchase a vessel of my own. I've some money in the banks and I should be able to secure a loan for the balance of the purchase."

"I assume you intend to seek Jackson's help with gaining cargoes?" Sumerford asked.

"Aye, and I've made other contacts in the Windwards through my service, it will be a meager living to begin with but with the war over, trade will flourish."

Sumerford smiled, "Ever the optimist," he said.

"Have you something to offer?" Donland asked.

Sumerford rubbed his chin and eyed Donland. He then pulled a case from his vest pocket and extracted one of his foul smelling cheroots. He tapped it on the table while still eyeing Donland. "As you know, I owned several vessels but I've sold them and therefore have no billet available at this time. However, an acquaintance has agreed to consider you for a billet if you were amenable to it."

Donland was tiring of Sumerford's cat and mouse game. "You have a proposal to put to me, I would that you make it and put an end to this."

"I have you attention, so I shall. It is this, *Hornet* is to be purchased and is to be assigned to protect the maritime interests of the United States. She will need a captain and a crew once the sale is complete. The captain will be sent from Boston but the crew is to be secured here. I've a master's authorization in my satchel with your name on it and orders from the Secretary of the Navy to assume temporary command of the newly commissioned vessel *Carolina*. They are yours to accept or to reject, what say you?"

"Huzza!" Honest shouted.

"What!" Donland exclaimed.

"I am authorized to grant you temporary command," Sumerford stated.

"How long is temporary?" Donland asked.

"Until the man is sent, it could be weeks or months, I can't predict the future but do not fret, in the meantime you will have what you now hold. You retain command over *Hornet*, is that not what you want?"

Donland's mind told him one thing but his heart told him another. "Yes, but not just until another man is sent and then I am cast onto the beach at his whim," he said.

Sumerford and Donland stared across the table at each other. Sumerford knew before he arrived that his friend would not be pleased with a temporary appointment. He had bent a few ears and all but twisted arms to have Donland appointed a lieutenant in the new navy but all to no avail. The best he could manage was the temporary command. Truth was that many in the new government did not trust him or any English captain.

"What is the length of the appointment as master?" Donland asked.

"No term!" Sumerford stated.

Donland thought for a moment and said, "I would have to resign my commission before accepting your offer. Which means going across to the fleet captain and presenting my resignation in writing. Once done, there is no turning back."

Sumerford could see the resistance in Donland's eyes.

"Isaac, times changed with the stoke of a pen in Paris, the war is over, the British navy is not what it was and your place in it is lost to you. If you hope to marry Betty, you need means to provide for her. Is that not so?"

Reluctantly Donland answered, "Aye."

Sumerford finally inserted the cheroot into his mouth and struck a match. He blew a stream of blue smoke.

The smell of the cheroot was, as ever, foul to Donland.

David finally decided to speak, "Sir, it is what you desire, is it not?"

Donland did not answer the boy, instead he rose from the chair and turned to the stern windows. His attention focused on *Stinger* sitting forlorn and for the time forgotten. His friend Powell was ashore with no prospects.

"What of Lieutenant Powell, he commanded *Stinger*, was he too offered temporary command as master?" Donland asked without turning.

"I recall him," Sumerford said. "No, he was not made an offer but it is within my authority to grant him temporary command. The vessel is to be purchased and therefore a crew must be engaged. I will make the offer to him if that is what you wish."

"Yes, do. He will be pleased to accept," Donland said.

"Will you then be pleased to accept?" Sumerford asked.

Donland turned and faced his friend. "Mathias, I am in your debt for your efforts. I am sure such was done in friendship and with sacrifice. But, such a decision is not to be made in haste. I will consider it and give you an answer in due course. How long do I have to decide?"

Mathias Sumerford twirled the cheroot in his mouth and removed it. His eyes were serious when he said, "Until I leave, which I plan to do once the paperwork is completed. No more than two days, I would imagine."

Donland did not hesitate, "You will have my decision on the day you depart if not sooner."

"Two days, then, I shall leave you to your deliberations. Will you dine with me tonight at the Three Crowns, say at eight?"

"Aye," Donland answered.

"You too David," Sumerford added and rose from the chair.

They followed Sumerford from the cabin and to the deck. Once there, Sumerford turned and said, "I've good memories of this ship as I trust you have. Let us hold them dear and part today as friends." He extended his hand to Donland.

The sun was edging over the horizon as Donland and David sat in the stern while being rowed across to the quay. David asked, "Isaac will you accept the offer?"

Donland did not look at the boy but rather stared ahead and considered his answer. "I've yet more time to consider but this I have concluded that you are old enough to make your own decisions. When I've decided, you will know before anyone. I would that you remain with me, but you are your own man. Fourteen years is young to some but they have not faced the guns and storms as you. Use your judgement and not allow your emotions to cloud it."

"Aye, so I've learned from you. When you reach your decision I shall make mine."

They sat in silence the remainder of the trip. The men at the oars were silent as well. Each of them knew change was coming, their fates were to be altered and their futures uncertain.

Powell greeted Donland at the entrance to the Three Crowns. He had waited just to greet Donland and share his good news. His purse was empty but his heart was full, he had employment.

"I've been invited to dine with you," Powell said.

Donland smiled and clapped Powell on the back, "I'm pleased, you've spoken with Sumerton then?"

Powell said, "You knew?"

"Aye," Donland said and added, "He has put the same to me."

"You will accept will you not?"

"Let us go in," Donland said to forestall having to answer.

The dining room was filled with mostly with men; the noise was considerable. Ignacio, the proprietor, said, "I have no tables, perhaps you came come back later?"

"We are to dine with Mister Sumerford, has he a table?" Donland asked.

"Si, he has engaged a separate room. Follow, please."

They followed across the main dining room to a side door that opened into a small room with one table. Sumerford was seated, as was Captain Symons who tasked by Pigot to reduce ships and men.

"Gentlemen, may I introduce Commander Donland and Lieutenant Powell," Sumerford said before the handshaking began.

The meal in the small room was uncomfortable for all. With only the one window it was ghastly hot. But it was not only the heat that brought discomfort, it was the company, Donland and Powell sat and hid their disdain for Symons. David was not introduced at all nor was he spoken to during the meal, he smiled when Symons departed and began to unbutton his coat.

"Will you accept the offer?" Sumerford asked while pouring brandy.

Donland held his glass for Sumerford to fill. He said, "Today is but one day and as you reminded me you can't predict the future. So, no I've not made a decision. But I am delighted that Commander Powell has accepted." He caught himself and said, "Lieutenant."

"Just Mister now," Powell corrected. "The higher ups have sealed my fate with the navy but thanks to Mister Sumerford I'm to stay afloat a little longer. And, if there is a berth in the new navy I shall avail myself."

"I would that you accept the offer, and I mean that sincerely," Sumerford said.

"Aye," Powell added.

Donland sipped his brandy and answered them, "Today the wind blows from the south but tomorrow it may blow from the west, it will not be known for fact until tomorrow which direction it will blow. The same holds true for fate; it is as fickle as the wind or a woman's love. I'd not wager money on the last or the second. Let us not speak any more of my decision."

Sumerford came aboard *Hornet* just after the noon sighting. He offered neither a warm greeting nor a cold one. Donland knew why he had come.

"It is done then?" he asked as they sat at the table in his cabin.

"It is, *Hornet* is now *Carolina* and as such I am to see to her needs. I've come to see if you will remain aboard or should I seek another to be master."

"I've made my decision and I shall be going ashore to report to Captain Hood, the flag captain. I fear there will be no orders but rather the letter of dismissal from active service. It will be a bitter pill but one expected."

My offer still holds," Sumerford stated.

"Aye," Donland acknowledged with a slight smile. "But, my heart will not allow my head to accept. I've known but one life as boy and man and another must be one of my choosing."

It was Sumerford's turn to smile. "Were you another man I'd say fool, but to you I say may fortune smile on you and the wind always be to your back."

"Thank you Mathias. May fate be kind to you as well."

Chapter Two

Captain Symons, a bulky man with thinning hair sat behind a table covered with maps and reports. "What the blazes now Watley?" He shouted to the flag lieutenant, Watley.

"Beg pardon, Sir, Commander Donland late of *Hornet*," Watley stated.

"Have you a report Lieutenant, if so leave it for it is to go to Captain Hood and not to me. You can hand it over to Lieutenant Watley and he will deliver it," Symons said and flipped a page in the book he held.

Donland went straight to the business at hand, "I've brought the account books from *Hornet.*"

Symons snapped, "Damn, leave them there by that stack. Be on your way!"

Watley caught Donland's elbow and tugged.

Dutifully, Donland turned and followed the flag lieutenant from the cabin. He was too stunned to speak.

"I've a letter for you," Watley said and produced a sealed envelope from inside his coat.

Donland took the letter and stared questioningly at the lieutenant.

"You better read it," Watley said.

Donland pulled the wax seal free and opened the letter. Admiral Pigot signed the single sheet. He began to read, "Lieutenant Donland is ordered to report to Captain Sheffield commanding *Brune*. Duties to be determined by Captain Sheffield."

Surprise was evident on Donland's face. Watley commented, "Not what you were expecting." He smiled.

Still stunned Donland managed, "no."

Brune was a smart twenty-four-gun frigate from the Portsmouth yard. She was, as frigates go, a thoroughbred with speed, strength and endurance. Donland had often gazed upon her lovely lines with desire. He could only imagine what sort of man would be given such a beauty to command.

Sheffield was a tall gangly man nearer forty than thirty with a long sharp nose and spoke with a booming voice. He received Donland in *Brune's* main cabin. "Wine or something stronger?" Sheffield asked after the pleasantries.

"Wine if you please, sir," Donland answered

The manservant poured wine into two small goblets.

"Sheffield noticed that Donland eyed the goblets and said, "Gifts from by sister, she knows nothing of ships." He studied Donland for a moment and changed tack, "I see you still wear your epaulette, pity you could not retain it but in these times any berth is better than being ashore. Which brings me to why you are here and not ashore. The admiral has ordered me to take you aboard to act as guide. Seems I'm to undertake a rescue and you are aquatinted with the town and surroundings. As that the war has ended and we are at peace with Spain, I'm to effect the rescue without incurring the ire of the Dons. So, here you are."

Donland could not believe his ears. He was to be nothing more than a guide, he had hoped for more, much more.

As if reading Donland's thought Sheffield said, "I've a full complement and lack not even for a midshipman. You will be a supernumerary only."

At least I know my place, Donland thought. He asked, "The place where I am to guide you, held by Spain is it?"

"Aye, Puerto Rico, Luquillo is the name of the place, you know it?"

"Aye, I know the place and the approaches by sea and land from the east and the south. Will you go in under sail?"

"No, it would be best if the Dons were not aware of our presence. The plan is to send you and a party ashore to make the rescue and to depart without the Dons any the wiser as to who snatched their prisoner."

"And who is the prisoner?" Donland asked.

"That I can't tell you," Sheffield said. "You will know before you are landed. If it were my decision I would tell you but I am under strict orders not to tell anyone until you are to be landed. Therefore, I assume and you should as well, that the party is valuable to the crown. Enough so, that this is to be done swiftly and secretly. There will be no glory and no mention in the Gazette."

Donland stated what was in his mind, "And when done, I will be put ashore on half-pay."

"That I'd not know," Sheffield said flatly.

Donland lifted the small goblet of wine, examined and set it down. "When do you sail?"

"Now," Sheffield answered. "Lieutenant Parker, my first, will see to your needs."

"Sir, I've a midshipman and my cox'un still aboard *Hornet*, I will need them for they too know the town and will of great benefit to me and to you. With your permission I will fetch them straight away."

Sheffield said firmly, "I think not!"

Donland was not to be put off, "This task, you say is on your head. If it is to be accomplished, local knowledge is going to be invaluable. Not just to lead your men to the town but to be able to find the place where your person is being held. We'll not have much time to do so before being discovered. With my midshipman and cox'un I can locate the person much quicker and without exposure until necessary. I deem it better to make use of all resources to insure success, do you not?"

Sheffield drummed his fingers on the table for a moment. "Very well, I will send a boat to fetch them. You, out of caution, will remain aboard here."

"That is acceptable," Donland stated and picked up the goblet of wine and drank.

Donland leaned against the bowsprit and watched the comings and goings of the harbor. He watched with great interest as sails were rigged on *Stinger*. Powell would be preparing her for her new captain; it was not a task that would be to Powell's liking. Nor would it be to his. This berth was also not to his liking but he welcomed an opportunity to be of use. Better a guide, he thought, than to have Powell's duty. At least he had opportunity whereas Powell had none. In either case, the two of them would doubtless be ashore and their naval careers ended.

He dared not turn to study *Hornet*. She, like *Stinger*, would be preparing for her new captain. There were a number of unemployed lieutenants on the beach that Sumerford could employ without difficulty. An opportunity to serve as master would feed them and provide for other needs. He did not fault Sumerford for the turn of events, better the man make a profit and find service for *Hornet* than she sit and rot. It would not be a fitting end to the valiant little sloop. She had been his, how his heart ached for her and to be dashing through the waves and troughs.

From amidships came the sounds of a boat bumping along side. Donland turned to see Honest and Simon follow David onto deck. They each in turn saluted the flag. David saw him and smiled before placing his hat back on his head. *How tall the boy had grown?* Donland thought. They had endured so much together, the fight to take *Morgador*, the hurricane on the island, treason and sickness. They both had come to love Betty Sumerford and to be loved by her.

David spoke to a midshipman on deck and then started for the bow. "Sir, are we to join?" he asked.

Donland answered, "No, we are to be borne as supernumeraries only. Once we have assisted in a task we are to return here. I will tell you more once Captain Sheffield confides in me. For the present, do as you are ordered and be amenable to all."

"Aye, sir," David answered. He glanced back at Honest and said, "We brought your dunnage aboard. Honest packed your other possessions and made arrangements for them to be stored ashore. We assumed we would not be returning to *Hornet*."

Donland sighed, "Just as well and I believe you to be correct in your assessment. It seems you, as I, have made your decision as to your future."

"Aye, it wasn't difficult," David answered.

"Then you best go below and stow your dunnage," Donland said.

"Aye," David replied and turned to go below.

Jackson was not a happy man; the cargo was half what was promised. He had tried to supplement it before sailing but to no avail. They had sailed from Guadeloupe with only twenty barrels of sugar instead of forty as he had contracted for. He had a choice, either put in at Saint Martin to purchase more sugar at higher prices or sail on to Anguilla and hope to supplement his cargo with rice, cotton or molasses. The likelihood of filling his hold this late in the season was not good.

"Owens trim that for'galnt!" Jackson shouted.

"Aye, sir!" Owens answered while eyeing the mast with disdain.

16

Jackson turned his back to the man. Owens was a liar and not to be trusted. The same, he found to be true of the other twelve men he had signed aboard. His original crew was caught up in a drunken brawl and his first mate and two others were killed. He was forced to find replacements and thought those cast on the beach by the navy would welcome a berth with decent pay. He had been wrong. Once he reached Savannah, he would be done with this lot and free to sign on men willing to work for honest wages.

Folly rolled on the swells. She was a poor sailor even on a calm sea. Jackson was accustomed to her ways, she was his and he was thankful for her. Were it not for Donland's generosity, he'd not have her. He remembered their parting; it had been difficult for they had shared success and failure aboard *Hornet*. There had been times when he'd not thought he'd not see another day but Donland brought them though. And, to be fair he had done for Donland on morn' one occasion. But it was the wounding that had changed his life and led to parting from *Hornet*. He wasn't the man he had been and *Hornet* needed a fit man as first officer. He jumped at the chance to have *Folly* as his own; it was earned and owed to him after the years of storm, fighting and hardship. It had been the right decision, for had he not taken *Folly*, he'd be on the beach with the rest of the castoffs. Fitting, aye, that was so, to have his own little *Folly*.

"Bishop, I'm going below, keep a sharp eye out," Jackson announced to the helmsman.

"Aye," Bishop said and spit a steam of tobacco.

Jackson sat down at the table in his cabin and poured a tankard of rum. He drank, he knew he was drinking too much but he drank all the same. The life of an island trader was not as much to his liking as he had hoped. He missed the hard discipline of a king's ship. He was not physically able to take the men aboard *Folly* to task as he should. They defied him and he was certain they laughed behind his back, especially when he was beset with coughing fits. These men did not fear him and were it not for the two pistols in his belt they would be unmanageable. Were *Folly* a king's ship and he master and commander, they'd fear the cat well enough. But it was not, *Folly* was his and he was master and a weak one at that. He needed a strong mate, a man he could trust and who would make the crew toe the line.

"Captain Sheffield wants you below," Lieutenant Parker announced.

"Aye," Donland acknowledged without the annoyance he felt. He decided not to let it show. He would not let on to Parker nor to Sheffield his feelings. The officer's lack of decency and respect for him aboard *Brune* appalled even the ordinary seamen. Donland had seen it in their faces. They at least had shown proper respect. Even so, Parker was more decent than *Brune's* third lieutenant Carstairs who in Donland's estimation, would be the death of many a sailor if he lived.

"Sir," Donland said and saluted as the marine sentry opened closed the door.

"Yes, I've been examining the charts. In my opinion, landing my boats along the coast you suggested would put the ship in unfavorable waters. There are shoals and dangerous reefs to the east and to the north. It will take a day for us to come round to Luquillo. By such time, the landing party could be compromised and I would be unable retrieve them. So, I will send the boats ashore at Cape San Juan, the trek will be no more than ten miles. Lieutenant Carstairs will lead the party and you will be under his command. If there are watchers he will have sufficient force to subdue them."

Donland held his temper and pretended to be studying the chart. He chose to be tactful, "Aye, sir, no more than ten miles but it will be through mostly swamps and marshes. I would guess it will take about a half day to traverse."

"Perhaps, but that will still leave you a half day to find the prisoner and signal me to enter the anchorage. It is such a small hamlet that it should be no problem for you to locate the prisoners. I would think Lieutenant Carstairs will be back aboard before nightfall."

"Sir!" the word escaped from Donland's lips before he could capture it.

"You object to my plan Mister Donland?"

Donland managed to hold his tongue. He looked from Sheffield to the map and then back to Sheffield. He pointed to the map and said, "There are batteries guarding the anchorage. Pirates and privateers still frequent Luquillo with the Dons consent. I fear that if *Brune* enters without permission she will be regarded unfavorably and may come under fire."

"They dare not!" Sheffield said and continued, "If they do what follows will be on their heads! If they fire it will be an act of war, we are at peace but that would be dashed and the Dons know it!"

"That be so Captain Sheffield but the cutthroats would see *Brune* as a threat and would bring guns to bear."

"Then I shall blow them out of the water and to hell!"

Donland sensed he was only antagonizing Sheffield. He said, "Aye, sir."

"Day after tomorrow at dawn then, *Brune* will be in position off Cape San Juan. You best follow my plan and succeed or not return. I'll brook no insubordination from you, do you understand?"

So there it was; Donland was not mistaken of the threat.

"Aye, sir," he answered.

David, Honest and Simon stood together amidships on the port side watching the vanishing coast line as *Brune* gathered wind in her sails. Honest knuckled his forehead in salute as Donland approached. "A fair day for sailing Captain," he said.

"Aye," Donland agreed without any hint of joy in his voice.

"Where we bound, I've not been told," David wanted to know.

Donland looked cautiously over his shoulder and came in close to the small group. He answered David in a low voice just loud enough for them to hear, "Puerto Rico, back to Luquillo to rescue a prisoner. Ask no questions but stay close to me when we are landed." He stepped away from them and continued toward the bow.

David and Honest exchanged curious looks at each other.

Simon asked, "Is Captain Donland in trouble?"

Honest smiled and answered, "I believe we are all in trouble. You mind your manners and be seen as little as possible."

"I shall do the same," David added for measure.

Chapter Three

Donland found solace in staring at the open sea. *Brune* was a fast and agile sailor due to her newly coppered hull. He once held out hope to command such a frigate but with each passing day that hope faded. Peace with France, Spain and the Americans dashed those hopes. When there is no war to be fought there is little need of fleets and armies. Those who were employed in such were without skills and means to earn a decent living, as they were viewed as undesirables and unemployable. Most would return to childhood homes only to discover they no longer had a place and would turn to drink and thieving. Ruined men and ruined lives all for king and country.

"Deck there! Frigate three points off the port bow!"

Donland instantly turned in the direction the lookout had called. He did not see her; he forgot his brooding.

"Don!" the lookout called down.

Donland craned his neck and just caught sight of what he thought was the tip of a mast.

For a brief moment, the others on deck were interested but soon resumed their tasks. There was no danger for there was no war. Two ships passing on a calm sea and each with peaceful intentions.

Donland continued to watch and soon saw sails and yards. The Spaniard was sailing on a converging tack. By the set her sails, he estimated that she would pass well ahead of *Brune* if she did not choose another tack. In his mind, he pictured a chart of the West Indies and concluded the Spaniard would tack for there was no logical destination on her current tack. He smiled as he thought of the Spanish captain thumbing his nose at his former enemy.

The ship's bell rang and the boatswain blew his shrill whistle. Donland turned from watching the Spaniard.

The drum began to beat to quarters. Men scampered up the ladders and then up the shrouds to take their sail-handing positions. From below decks came the clamor of more men rushing to their gun stations. Hatches were secured, lashings rechecked, boats were unlashed and made ready to sway out for towing. The drum continued to beat as the marines assembled, the sergeant pushing and cursing made quite a spectacle.

Then Sheffield came up; he looked every bit the strutting peacock. He went straight to the quarterdeck and was handed a glass, which he put to his eye. Lowering it he snapped it shut. "Lieutenant Parker I'll have the larboard guns readied!" He shouted.

Donland could not believe his eyes or ears. The fool was giving provocation to the Spaniard. A drill was one thing but this was an unnecessary show of force, one that could easily be misinterpreted.

The Spaniard came on. Her bow wave of foaming white water indicated that she was not perturbed or threatened by Sheffield's show of force.

Donland wondered what Sheffield was playing at. The Spanish frigate carried forty guns almost double that of *Brune* and with one broadside would surely devastate *Brune* leaving her a broken ruin.

"Deck there! Yards going round!" The lookout shouted down to the deck.

In a flash, as Donland watched, the Spanish frigate went about. It was a superb show of seamanship by the Spanish crew.

"Huzzah! Huzzah! Huzzah!" *Brune's* crew cheered.

"Silence there!" Parker bellowed.

Sheffield said something to Parker and they both laughed.

Parker replied, "Aye, sir!" and Sheffield started for the hatch.

"Remain at stations!" Parker shouted and the order was relayed through the ship.

They remained at their stations until the Don's sails disappeared over the horizon.

Donland watched and listened and was disturbed by Sheffield's actions. The man was a fool inviting disaster. The sooner he was off the ship and away from the man the better.

David lay in his hammock in deep sleep. He awoke with a start as a hand shook him. It seemed he had only just climbed into the hammock after being told that he was to be on deck before dawn.

"It's time," Honest said in the dark.

"Aye," David answered and began to gather his wits.

Donland was waiting on deck with Simon and Honest. David joined the trio and the four of them stood together as the first boat was lowered.

Carstairs came forward from the quarterdeck and said, "The four of you will go in the first boat with ten men and I will follow in the second boat. Once we are landed I will send the bulk of the men and the boats back. Hold your tongues and take nothing upon yourselves. Wait for me before you even think about venturing inland."

Donland was already in a foul mood and Carstairs' self-importance deepened the mood. "As you wish," Donland said back to Carstairs.

23

Brune coasted along under light sail with a quarter moon sinking. The stars were still bright but there was a glowing hint of sunrise coming. It was still too dark to make out the coastline and in Donland's opinion, it was dangerous to be closing with an unknown coastline. He well remembered the many shoals along this coast and with each passing storm those shoals shift. But whatever befell *Brune*, Sheffield would be the one held accountable.

"Brail up all sail Mister Parker," Sheffield ordered.

"Aye, Captain!" Parker bellowed his orders.

Men sprang into action and the captain of the top began cursing and prodding his mates along the toe-ropes. Men along the deck hauled on lines bracing up the yards.

"Quiet on deck!" Parker shouted.

The men ceased their cursing and badgering.

Without sail *Brune* coasted along until her way came off her.

"No steerage!" the helmsman cried.

Donland gripped the rail and peered into the darkness. If there were a coastline, he could not make out any feature. He thought he faintly heard the crash of waves. There was no hint of breakers even with the faint pale light of the sinking moon.

"Twenty minutes till first light," Goodsen the sailing master said loudly enough to carry the length of the ship.

Brune rolled on the sea and from time to time there was a clink of metal on metal somewhere below deck. It seems not a man breathed.

The lookout's call startled everyone, "Breakers off the port bow!"

"Over the side, Mister Carstairs!" Sheffield ordered.

Donland sighed; it had begun. He said to David, "Sit by me! Keep your power dry!"

"Aye, sir," David answered and followed Donland down to the boat.

By the time they were settled into the boat, Donland thought he saw a tinge of pink beginning in the eastern sky. The oarsmen waited for the second boat to be loaded. Donland gave the order, "Stoke!"

The oarsmen obeyed and began maneuvering the boat away from the hull. They began to pull.

"How far do you make it sir?" the boat captain asked.

"Two miles," Donland answered.

"Fair long pull!" the boat captain remarked.

"Aye," Donland agreed.

He turned and had no difficulty seeing and hearing Carstairs' boat trailing fifty yards behind. It was the larger of the two boats and would have difficulty maintaining the pace of the smaller boat. Donland smiled to himself. He wanted to be ashore before Carstairs' boat was near.

"Current running strong from behind us," the boat captain said.

"How strong?" Donland inquired.

"I make it a good three knots if not four," the man answered.

Donland considered the information. For the boats it was good news but for *Brune*, it could spell disaster. The tide and drift of the current were carrying *Brune* to the northeast and toward danger. Sheffield should anchor and wait until dawn to get underway. Donland remembered the long reef with an extended shoal. In the dark, *Brune* would strike before anyone was aware of the danger. Donland remembered the difficulty the Spaniards encountered as they chased after *Hornet*. *Brune's* draft was considerably greater than *Hornet's* and was at great risk of running aground if caution were not exercised.

Dawn was breaking as Donland's boat reached the breakers. The small beach was deserted and beyond the beach was the murky dark jungle. Donland stood just before the boat reached the breakers and scanned up and down the coast. Their landing was at least a half-mile to the west of where Sheffield had planned for them to land. He turned and saw that *Brune* was no more than a mile behind. The current and tide were pushing her inland toward the shoaling. Her sails were slack and the light wind was continuing to push her toward the shoal. *Brune* would have difficulty holding enough wind to regain steerage.

25

"Breaker sir!" the boat captain shouted.

Donland sat just as the boat crested the wave. The oarsmen timed their next stroke and the boat shot forward into the foaming surf. The boat was soon grounded and two men leapt over the gunnel and began pulling the boat into shallow water.

Some ten feet from the wet sand Donland ordered, "Landing party ashore!"

He leapt over the side and began wading to the beach. The water was just below his knees and spray from crashing waves sent spray into his face. He took a moment to turn and check on the progress of the second boat. What he saw did not surprise him, Carstairs was heading back to the frigate. Donland didn't question why, he knew. *Brune* was grounded on the shoal. Sheffield was ordering the boats back to kedge her off the shoal.

"We're to return?" the boat captain asked.

"Aye, Captain Sheffield will need the boat to get her off," Donland answered.

He studied the small group of men, "you two," he said to two of the younger men, "stay with me."

The two looked at each other and the one with dark hair and the beginnings of a beard answered, "Aye."

The second man sounded reluctant but answered, "Aye,"

Donland instructed the boat captain. "Tell Captain Sheffield that I will seek out the prisoner and be ready to rejoin as we agreed," "Aye, sir," The man answered and added, "If we get off that bloody shoal by then!"

Donland set off with Honest, David, Simon with the two sailors from *Brune* following. When he reached the tree line he stopped and asked, "What are your names?"

"Dobbs, sir," the one with the scraggly beard answered.

"Williamson," the second answered.

Honest said, "Captain, I will go up the beach and see if there is a track."

"Aye," Donland answered and said to Dobbs and Williamson, "You two go down the beach. Call out if you find a track."

"Aye, sir," Dobbs answered and the two set off.

There was coolness coming from the jungle beyond the tree line. "You two wait there in the shade, I will remain here so I can see Honest and the other two," Donland said to Simon and David.

The sun was now well up and the heat of its rays began making Donland sweat. He knew the jungle would soon loose the coolness of the night and he hoped to enter the town well before then. He did not envy the men in the boats trying to work *Brune* free. It would be a backbreaking task and it should have been avoided. He would have but then, he would not have chosen to land on this coast.

Honest began to wave signaling he had found a track.

"Simon," Donland called.

"Aye, sir," Simon answered and came from the trees.

"Run down the beach to Dobbs and Williamson and bring them back."

"Aye, sir," the boy answered and set off at a run.

Donland stepped into the shade of the trees where David sat on fallen tree. "We'll be off once they reach us."

"Who are we to rescue?" David asked.

Donland answered with a question, "Would you believe I've only a first name?"

"All this for a man with no name!" David said incredulously.

"Aye, but a relation of some noble that the crown holds dear. He was taken along with the packet that was bound for Jamaica."

"Held for ransom?" David asked.

Donland smiled and said, "I've not been told that detail but I would assume so. The young noble probably bragged of his relationship."

"Were it me, I'd not so," David said.

"No, you would not, I credit you with more wisdom than that. But, a relation of the crown, he'd not be that wise."

"You think all nobility are so full of themselves?"

"Aye," Donland answered truthfully.

The boom of a cannon broke the calm. Birds immediately took flight squawking as they did so.

No more than three seconds later a second shot boomed and was followed by a third.

"A battery, sir?" David asked.

"Aye," Donland answered. "It was as I feared. *Brune* is aground and that battery we fought has been restored and are ranging on her."

"But we are at peace with the Dons are we not?" David asked.

"Aye, at peace with them but not the pirates that remain at Luquillo. They'll knock *Brune* to splinters in time if she does not free herself. She'll not receive aid from the Dons either."

David asked, "What of us if she is destroyed?"

Donland sighed, "We shall find the lad, free him and return to Antigua the best way we can. Captain Sheffield, I fear will not be of assistance."

"Why not?"

Donland turned as he heard the footsteps of Dobbs, Williamson and Simon returning. He said to David in a whisper, "Having taken fire, he will abandon us and blame me for putting the ship at risk."

David was aghast, "He wouldn't!"

"Aye, he would, it is his way. No more talk of this."

To the others he said, "Honest has found a track, we will join him. Stay close in to the trees so that you're not seen by those at that battery."

Halfway to where Honest waited Williamson said, "They hit her!"

Donland did not reply, there was nothing he could do. He considered attempting to take the battery but with only four pistols among them it would be an empty gesture. No, *Brune* would have to continue to receive fire until she could free herself. Many might die and the ship might be lost but there was naught he could do. The task was to free the prisoner and that he would do.

The track that Honest found was nothing more than that, it wound through the jungle barely wide enough for a man. They could hear the boom of cannon even in the thick foliage and with each shot Donland wondered if the boats were making any headway in freeing the stranded frigate. He would not know until they reached the town.

They were half-mile inland when they came upon a well-used path running east and west. "This way," Donland said and led off. The boom of cannon still came; sometimes the firing was in twos and at other times threes. Each man knew that with each shot that *Brune* was taking damage. And each wondered just how much damage she could endure.

They followed the jungle trail for a half-mile and it joined a road. It was the road Donland remembered from when they had crossed from Fajardo on the southern coast.

"I make it another two miles?" Donland said to Honest.

"Aye, sir but perhaps less," Honest answered.

Donland halted the small group. It was time to split them up. "We will split into three parties," he announced. "Dobbs you will go with me, Willamson you'll go with Mister Welles and Honest you and Simon travel as before. We are seeking captured English sailors, tell no one what you are about. Go into the pubs and the cafes and strike up conversations. If any one asks, tell them you are Americans and became stranded on the island when your ship sailed without you. You can give any reason you like as to why you were left, it matters not. Move the conversation to dislike for the English and that jail is too good for those who are captured. If they mention something like, "yes, and those in that house at the top of the hill ought to be hung," then find me immediately, understand?"

"Aye," they each said.

Donland pulled his purse from his trousers. "You'll need coin for rum, so take this. We've not but half a day to find the prisoners and free them. We are to rejoin *Brune* in the evening."

"If she's still afloat," Dobbs mused.

"Aye, and if not we shall have to make our own way. Our meeting place will be at the small stable near the stone house, both Mister Welles and Honest know it." Donland answered. "Mister Welles lead off. Honest and Simon will follow in a quarter-hour."

"Aye, sir," David answered.

Donland waited another quarter-hour before he set off. They walked along the road in silence until Donland came upon the track leading down to the battery. He halted and realized he'd not heard a gun in some time. "Dobbs we will go down this trail, it leads to that battery. I've not heard a gun fire for some time and I think we should investigate *Brune's* progress."

"Aye," Dobbs answered and followed Donland down the trail.

When Donland heard Spanish voices he halted. There was laughter and more conversation. He caught only a few words that he understood and decided against going closer to the men. He turned to Dobbs and pointed toward the beach and angled away from the battery.

They were careful to make as little noise as possible as they wound their way between bushes, vines and trees. The jungle was thick and they made slow progress. Both men were soaked to the skin with sweat when they finally emerged onto the beach.

"There sir," Dobbs said and pointed.

It was *Brune* a mile or more distance. She was not under sail and at that distance they could not hear or tell what was happening on her decks.

"Taken or abandoned," Donland mused aloud.

"Aye, I'd give a gold guinea to know which," Dobbs said.

"Right Dobbs, but we've no way to know. If I had a glass, even a small one it would tell the tale, but I've not. Let us be away, we'll stay close to the trees."

"Aye, sir," Dobbs answered and walked abreast of Donland. Both occasionally turned to stare at *Brune* hoping to see sails set.

Chapter Four

They came in the night. He sensed them but it was too late. He opened his eyes just in time to see the swing of the belaying pin. He awoke in the bow of the jolly boat adrift on an empty sea. Two others were with him and neither stirred, he wondered if they were dead. He sat up and scanned the empty sea. *Folly* was lost to him.

Jackson's head hurt and his tongue was thick in his dry mouth. He saw no food or water in the boat. There was not even an oar. He knew the reason; they were to be left for dead. He kicked the man's foot that was nearest him. The man did not stir, he kicked again. The man groaned but did not rise. Jackson kicked him again and managed to croak, " Wake up blast you!"

The man's head lolled and he attempted to get his hands under him and rise but failed.

Jackson kicked the man again and once more for good measure.

The name the man had given when Jackson signed him on was John Scott. He said that he had been a gunner aboard *Stinger* and gained a berth with a merchantman after she had paid off.

The master of the merchantman withheld half his pay so he came aboard *Folly*. Bishop hadn't taken to him. It was reason enough for Bishop to cast him aside and into the boat. Jackson kicked Scott again

This time Scott stirred and opened his eyes. He immediately shaded his eyes against the harsh sun. Seeing Jackson he asked, "What?"

"We've been cast adrift," Jackson managed through his swollen lips. "No water and no food, no oars either."

"Gwad!" Scott said and sat up rubbing his head. "Where are we?"

"In a bad way," Jackson said and gripped the gunnel. He stood and slowly searched the sea. To the west he saw what he thought was a purple smudge, perhaps a distant island. He looked down at the man lying in the bow. O'Rouke, the Irishman who claimed he could lick any man with only one fist appeared to be dead.

"See if you can rouse him," Jackson said to Scott. "If not we'll put him over the side after we strip him."

Scott readjusted himself but did not rise. He then shook O'Rouke by the arm. "Wake up you or over the side with you!"

O'Rouke's body shook but did not respond.

Scott raised himself then slapped O'Rouke on the face.

O'Rouke did not open his eyes but said, "Do that again laddie and I'll break ye in half!"

Jackson smiled and looked again in the direction of the island.

"Alright then, let us be at it. We'll rip out this bench for a paddle. There's land to the west no mor'n ten miles and with this wind we'll make it about dark."

O'Rouke sat upright and stretched his neck. He stared at Jackson and said "Aye, and then a boat and then some killing."

"Aye," Jackson agreed. "We'll find that bastard Bishop and take turns with the knife on him!"

They were fortunate that O'Rouke had his knife. They used it to split the bench seat into two pieces thus having two paddles instead of one. Two hours and many blisters later, Jackson handed his half of the split board to Scott. The hours of paddling with no water took a heavy toll. Jackson slumped onto the floorboards. "Just a bit of rest," he said before his eyes closed.

He awoke an hour later. Scott and O'Rouke occasionally stroked with the paddles. The island lay ahead about another mile. Wind and current had done more to close the distance than their paddling. Thirst and the sun consumed their energy forcing their strokes to be without strength. Occasionally, each man scooped a handful of water just to moisten his lips. Being sailors, they knew the danger of doing so but with the island in sight, they took the risk.

"Another hour lads," Jackson said and took O'Rouke's paddle. His first strokes were strong but those that followed were mere feeble attempts. "They've not seen us yet." It was the last thing Jackson said until he came to and saw stars overhead and sand beneath him. The rhythmic crash of waves told him that he had survived.

Scott was aware that Jackson stirred and said, "We've no fire, but we've some water." He raised Jackson's head and squeezed water from a rag into Jackson's mouth. "I thought you was a goner but O'Rouke said you was too damn mad to die. I figure he was right."

The little water did nothing to quench Jackson's thirst. He asked through cracked, swollen lips, "How much water?"

"Found a log with some, not much but enough to get us through the night. O'Rouke and me will find more when the sun comes up. You rest easy now."

Jackson asked, "A few more drops?"

"Aye," Scott answered and held up the rag again and squeezed a few more drops.

O'Rouke was awakened in the night by thunder. At first he thought it was the sound of a broadside then there was a bright flash of lightning with a sharp crack of thunder. He rose up on

34

one elbow, and saw Jackson sitting up. Scott was likewise sitting up.

The rain fell in a torrent. Jackson and the other two men lay with their mouths open. The torrent slackened to drizzle and soon dissipated. Jackson was instantly cold and shivered. He stood and removed his shirt and trousers. The water was not to be wasted so he held his shirt above his mouth and twisted and squeezed until not a drop remained. It was foul tasting with salt but it satisfied.

"Day soon," Jackson said.

"Aye, and I'll have my breakfast," O'Rouke quipped.

Donland sat in the shade of a large sprawling oak watching the stone building. It was as the same place the pirates had used to imprison the English sailors when he had led the previous rescue. As before, there were two men armed men with pistols and swords on each side of the double doors. But unlike before, there were three men seated under a canvas awing in the alley between the house and the stone building.

He reasoned that taking all five of the men in broad daylight was out of the question. The attempt would have to be made at night. Until night fell he and the others would be vulnerable.

It was then that he saw Simon and Honest making their way along the street toward the stone building. He was certain they saw him and was pleased they did not acknowledge him. They continued on past the stone building and disappeared down a side street. No doubt Honest was going to check the security at the rear of the building.

Rising, he spotted Dobbs coming toward him carrying what appeared to be a bag. He started toward Dobbs on the opposite side of the street in hopes that the guards would not notice their meeting.

"What have you Dobbs?" Donland asked.

"It's old but it'll do," Dobbs said and pulled a rag off the telescope he was holding. It was old, dented but made of metal not wood.

"Where'd you get it?" Donland asked.

"Stole it," Dobbs answered. "Shop down by the beach had lots of old swords and such, most likely stole from someplace else."

"Aye, taken off some ship looted by pirates," Donland said as he took the glass from Dobbs. He lifted it to his eye and looked down the street. The lens was cloudy but not cracked, it would serve his purpose.

"Let's go down to the beach and see what has happened to *Brune*," Donland said as he wrapped the glass in the rag.

Even without the glass Donland saw several small boats surrounding *Brune*. He lifted the glass to his eye and focused, There was a whiff of smoke as one of the small boats fired either a swivel gun or a small cannon. *Brune* appeared still stuck on the bar. "She'll not get off and they'll have her," Donland said with the glass still to his eye.

"You think so sir?" Dobbs asked.

"Aye," Donland said and lowered the glass. "They have blasted *Brune*'s boats with swivel guns and she's stuck fast. We'll have no help from that quarter. It will be best if we keep our distance from those taken off or we'll end up as prisoners."

"May I see, sir?" Dobbs asked.

"Aye," Donland replied and handed the glass to Dobbs. Dobbs squinted and said, "She's no hope!"

"Little or none," Donland said and started back up the beach with Dobbs at his side.

A blast caused them to turn and Dobbs lifted the glass. "There's a fire on her deck!" he said in a whisper.

Donland reached and took the glass from Dobbs. He saw the fire on *Brune*'s deck, the lens then filled with gray and blue and for a moment he was not sure what he was seeing and then the rolling thunder of the explosion caught his ears. He lowered the glass to see that *Brune* had no masts. He lifted the glass again and was able to see clearly that *Brune's* lovely figure was marred with severe damage to her quarterdeck, gunnels and railings. She had blown up and as he watched there were huge splashes around her as debris rained down.

"Some fool touched off the magazine!" Dobbs shouted.

"Fire," Donland answered while studying the wreckage. He turned his glass onto the small boats. Two were empty and there was no movement aboard the others.

"There will be few prisoners, such a blast gets most of them, the water and sharks will have the rest," Donland said and lowered the glass. "We will inform the others of events when we meet them later."

"What of us, sir? What are we to do now that we have no ship?" Dobbs asked.

"What we came to do Dobbs, free the prisoner and return to Antigua. The how of both will come about as events unfold. It may take some time but it would seem we have time." Donland answered and added, "One thing is certain, there will be no rescue. Let us go into the town and discover what we may."

"Aye, sir," Dobbs answered and turned for one last look at *Brune*.

David and Williamson lounged against a tree in front of the stone building. They pretended to ignore Donland as he approached but he went straight to them with Dobbs in tow. "Follow at a distance," Donland whispered in passing and continued on to the stable.

The stable was as Donland remembered, small and stank of cow and sheep manure. It was not a good hiding place in daylight but it would do for the meeting. David entered first.

"*Brune* will not be rescuing us," Donland stated once Williamson had entered. "She went aground and received heavy fire. Boats were sent out and in the course of the fight the magazine was fired. I fear she is lost, as are her officers and company. We will be on our own but I intend to complete the task. Have you any information Mister Welles?"

"Captain we've not discovered very much of anything. I'm fairly certain that there are no prisoners in the stone building. Some men came with a handcart filled with small casks, the kind that hold powder. I stood across the street and watched them carry the casks into the building. If there had been prisoners, I'd have seen them. They hardly paid me attention."

Williamson added, "Aye, I seen the casks too, ain't no men in there."

"Anything else?" Donland asked.

"Not much except that I seen quite a few lads about I'd know to be tars, don't none speak like the Dons," Williamson said.

Donland was pleased with that bit of information. They would not be at risk for having their conversations overheard. "If you should be approached, tell them that you were stranded in Fajardo and came overland in search of another berth."

"Aye," David answered, as did Williamson.

"Very well, continue going about the town listening and watching the comings and goings. I will locate a house for us to sleep in and have our meals. We may be here a few days in order to complete our task and to gain the means of escaping the island. Let me assure you that we will do both for I have no intention of remaining here. Come here again at sunset, by then I will have secured a place to sleep."

"Aye, sir," David said.

Chapter Five

Donland found Honest and Simon sitting in the shade of a tree near the beach where fishermen landed their boats. At first they paid him no notice but once he sat on the sand and removed his hat they came over to him. "Anything?" he asked.

"Nothing as yet," Honest answered and asked, "Where's Dobbs?"

Donland grinned. "You heard the explosion?"

"Aye, we heard, magazine was it?"

"It was," Donland answered. "I've sent Dobbs to a café to listen to gossip. One man would be less suspicious. We've time to find the prisoners it seems."

Honest sat next to Donland. "We be marooned," he said in a woeful tone.

Donland could not help himself; he laughed. "Aye," he said and added, "Not the first time and if we live, not the last. But, we are still employed and still have orders. So, we will complete the task as it comes to us no matter if it is a week or more. Likewise, there will be means for leaving. I see that there are two ships sitting yonder, either would serve our purpose. Perhaps, in a day or two there will be another, perhaps more suitable to our needs."

Honest nodded and smiled. He picked up a hand full of sand and allowed it to run out between his fingers. "Time, we've that it seems."

Donland rose and smiled at Simon. He turned to Honest who was now standing. "Continue as you are. I'm off to find us a place to lodge for the night. We will meet at the stable at sunset."

"Aye," Honest replied leaving off the "sir".

The sun was dipping below the horizon as Donland made his way along the beach. He had spent the better part of two hours observing the comings and goings of boats. One of the two ships anchored in the roads was definitely a pirate vessel and the other a merchantman. He reasoned that both were not likely to remain more than a few days. The pirates would be in search of prey and the merchantman to sell his cargo of sugar. There would be others to take their place in the coming days.

He came upon a vacant one room house and inquired about it. The woman conveyed in broken English, "no man, no woman, gone!" It was only one room and no more than a shed but it would serve his purpose. They would have a place to sleep and a place to meet. The few coins remaining in his purse would last only a few days and it was food that would become a concern, one, which may lead to having to make rash decisions. He was not worried about Honest, David or Simon but the other two, he was not sure they could be counted on when hunger became uncomfortable.

They were all at the stable when he arrived. "Let us be going, I have a house," he announced. "We will go out in pairs, allow distance for there are watchers. The pirates control this town and they are wary of newcomers."

He went out first with Dobbs. The house was at the edge of the town near the road they had traveled. The squeal of pigs from the sty next to the house greeted Donland. He minded not their squeals but their stench was another matter. The breeze was blowing from their direction and he hoped it would turn in the night.

The little one-room house was as he last saw it. It held a small table, two chairs and a cot with a straw tick. The floor was dirt and the roof was composed of palm fronds. He fully expected it to leak when the rain came. But, it would do them for a few days.

David and Williamson arrived and Williamson glanced at the interior, "Reminds me of why I left me old dad's farm."

David added, "I'd not want to live here."

"Nor I," Donland answered and sat in the chair. "Sit and tell me of your day."

David sat. "I've no news of prisoners. We discovered two buildings that were being guarded; one I'm certain is for booty and the other the home of a rich merchant. Other than that I've little to tell. Perhaps, the prisoners are on that anchored ship. I set Williamson to watching it and he observed only four men on deck at any one time."

"Aye, sir, no more than an anchor watch," Williamson added from the cot.

Honest came in followed by Simon and Dobbs. Honest set a sack on the table and Dobbs placed a jug beside it.

"I've some yams, bit of rice and a bag of beans. The jug is poor man's wine; half water if I'm to guess. We'll not starve right off," Honest declared.

"Thoughtful of you Honest. I was going to send you out again to buy us some bread but with this lot we've enough for the night and breakfast," Donland said.

"Aye," Honest said and turned to Simon, "Fetch us some wood."

"You've nothing to cook in," Donland observed.

Honest smiled and reached into the sack and pulled out a small pot. "Fellow who sold me the wine gave me the pot. Seems there is no shortage of such."

41

"Pirates and privateers wouldn't value a rusted and dented pot, they prefer gold or silver," Donland mused.

"Aye, but this will do us for a night or two."

"With good fortune a night or two," David said and rose from the chair. "I'll help Simon with the wood."

Donland did not object, it was not fitting for a midshipman but the two were close friends and in this place both may as well be as equals. He lifted the jug of wine and drank. The sweet taste did little to disguise the vinegary taste. His face contorted into a frown and his mouth was dry. He lifted the jug once more and began pouring the contents onto the dirt floor.

Dobbs made to speak but Donland retorted, "Not fit for the swine and certainly not fit for man." With the jug empty, he rose. In his mind he thought, "if a midshipman can fetch firewood a lieutenant can fetch decent wine, bread and water."

"Dobbs, we will fetch some decent wine," Donland said.

"Aye, sir!" Dobbs answered with pleasure in his voice as he rose from the cot.

"Baked just this morning," the old woman said as Donland inspected the loaf in the lantern light. He saw no weevil holes and paid the woman two pennies for two loaves.

At the saloon he purchased three bottles of wine. The man opposed Donland first tasting the wine but relented when Donland turned to leave. The wine was at best decent. He handed the bottles to Dobbs who had refilled the jug with water.

The smell of a fire and simmering beans greeted Donland as he entered the house. David and Simon sat on the cot playing a guessing game. One would describe an object found aboard ship and the other had to guess. Donland smiled, "Home, sweet home," he said and removed his hat.

"Food's ready Isaac," Honest announced.

"Aye," Donland answered. He did not admonish Honest for not saying sir or captain. Honest knew, just as he did, that they were sure to have drawn someone's attention by now. The pirates would have their spies.

"We've no utensils or plates," Honest stated as he handed Donland a palm frond.

Donland grinned and said, "The Lord provides and His bounty is abundant. Not the first time I've eaten from such a plate, nor will it be the last if I live."

"Aye," Honest said and poured beans from the pot onto the frond. "Potatoes are in the fire, you best use your knife."

Simon and David sat on the cot, Honest and Donland had the chairs. Williamson and Dobss contented themselves with the dirt floor. No one spoke as they ate. The jug of water was passed around, as was one of the bottles of wine. There were no complaints and each was pleased to have a full belly after the long day.

"We've bread and beans enough for breakfast," Honest announced then asked, "What of tomorrow?"

"Fishing," Donland said. "We've got to eat," he added.

Honest was somewhat astonished and blurted, "fishing? What of....?

Donland silenced him by saying, "Aye and you best catch your share or you'll not eat!" He then put his finger to his lips.

"Aye," Honest said and nodded. "Fishing it will be and what of you?"

Donland said loudly, "I will inquire as to vessels for sale. We make no money on the land and there are prizes to be taken at sea."

Williamson and Dobbs faced each other.

"Aye," David said with understanding. "I'd do with some money in my pocket, there are some ladies I'd care to meet."

It was Donland's turn to be surprised, "You, bah, you would not know what to do with one."

David's reply was serious, "More'n you think."

Simon laughed and Honest turned to stare at his son.

Donland changed the topic of conversation. "Tomorrow, you fish and I go about the town."

Chapter Six

"So what are you?" Amos Spencer asked Donland.

"Thirty and fit," Donland answered.

"And you say you were a lieutenant?"

"Aye, was fourth on the *Medsua* under Captain Oakes, do you know her?"

"Aye, a few years back. Oakes I heard was killed."

"That is so, no loss there," Donland lied.

Spencer refilled the tankard in front of him with rum. He lifted and drank deeply.

Donland watched the heavy-jowled man. He didn't like him but like and dislike did not enter into the need for a ship.

Spencer appeared to be thinking. The man was crafty else he'd not own three ships. All three fitted out to capture unsuspecting merchantmen. Donland could only wait.

Spencer eyed Donland, set down the tankard and said, "Two days, aye, I will know in two days if I'll take you on. Be back here in two days."

Donland smiled and replied, "Aye, I'll be here."

He rose from the table and extended his hand. Spencer eyed it for a second, and waved Donland away.

Donland walked back in the direction of the house and as he did his eyes darted from side to side, slowing to hear snatches of conversation. David came from the house well before Donland reached it. A man holding a pistol to David's back followed him. Donland let them pass and drew his own pistol and jammed it into the man's back. "Lower it or you'll have no liver!"

"I'll kill him first," the man said.

"Then neither of us will gain anything," Donland answered and shoved the pistol hard.

The man, who stank of rum and filth, hesitated.

Donland withdrew the pistol from the man's ribs and clubbed him with the butt of the pistol. The man sank to his knees. "Catch him!" Donland said to David.

David turned and caught the man before he fell. Donland moved quickly and helped David to drag the unconscious man into the house.

"Who is he?" Donland asked.

"I don't know, I came back here to get some bread and water for Dobbs and Williamson. This fellow followed me in."

"Then we will wake him and gain some answers. Pour some water in his face, that'll stir him."

David picked up the jug and started to pour. The man stirred and jerked upright. He made to rise but Donland placed a foot in his stomach.

"Now who are you and why have you come?" Donland demanded.

The man looked up at Donland and the pistol. He blew a breath and said, "Thought the boy was one of them off the ship, Captain Morrison is paying for any of them that got away."

"And who is Morrison?" Donland asked.

"Captain of the *Charlotte,* she's anchored out there!" the man said with a jerk of his head.

Donland removed his foot and asked, "This Morrison, he runs the town too?"

"I'll not say," the man said.

The foot when back into the man's stomach. "You'll say or I'll mash your guts out!"

The man winced in pain but said nothing. Donland pressed harder.

The man attempted to knock Donland's foot away but Donland reacted swiftly with a blow of the pistol barrel across the man's nose. Blood spurted and the man's hand went to his nose to stem the flow. Donland removed his foot, squatted and drew his knife. "I'll cut it off! Tell me!"

The man shook his head while still holding his nose. He did not see the butt of the pistol coming, it struck him squarely on his crown and he went limp.

"Sir!" David exclaimed.

Donland stuck the pistol into his belt and faced David. "He told what he could, he'd not risk Morrison finding out he told. He's no use to us. But, you and Simon best beware, there will be others seeking a reward."

"Aye," David said with understanding. "What are you going to do with him?" he asked.

"You said you came for bread and water, you best take it now," Donland said without answering David's question.

David hesitated.

"Go, don't force me to order you!" Donland said firmly.

David collected the jug and the bread and went to the door. Donland followed him as far as the door. "Have they any luck?" he asked.

"Aye, a few." David said and turned away.

The man was heavy but Donland managed to drag him to the window at the back of the room and push him through it. He then went around the house and drug the man into the jungle. It was difficult getting him over roots and through the vines but he managed. When he reached a small clearing, he

drew his sword and hacked down on the man's neck. Blood
spurted from the cut vein and Donland watched until it stopped
pumping. He had killed many men, hacked them with sword and
dirk, when fighting. It was the first time he had killed a man who
could not defend himself. It sickened him but he knew it had to
be done. He told himself that the man was an enemy just as all
the others had been. Still, he regretted taking the life.

Donland, having disposed of the threat set off down the
street to find Morrison's house. He felt he should know it at
once, it would be guarded.

He took note of the high wall and iron gate as he walked
past the house. The gate was open and he was able to a portion
of the house. It was he imagined, a single-story, the outside
whitewashed and the roof red slate.

Several minutes later he returned on the opposite side of the
street hoping to find a suitable place to watch the entrance
without the guards becoming curious. The best he could do was
a café some three hundred yards away. He sat at an outdoor
table and ordered a glass of wine, spending money he could not
afford to spend.

The proprietor, a tall dark woman, came to him an hour
after sitting and politely asked if he wanted more wine. Donland
did not miss the tone she used which suggested that if he were
not buying then he was to move on. He moved on, the hour had
been without fruit. Since the house occupied a corner, he
decided to walk along the side street as far as the beach and then
return on the street to the back of the house. There were no
other entrances but there was a carriage maker's shop on the
corner opposite the house. He sat on the ground under the
shade of an oak with his back against the tree. There were
people about and those that passed paid him no attention. He
lingered an hour, nothing caught his attention so he stood and
returned to the street with the iron gates. Nothing had changed;

the two guards were the same. He concluded that watching the house during the day was fruitless, perhaps at night he might see or hear something. No doubt his time would be better spent fishing with the others.

He wandered into one café and saloon after another for another hour. Then decided a breath of sea air was in order. On the beach he was mildly surprised not to see any vessels. The plan he had been formulating to seize an anchored vessel and escape was dashed. But, so was the plan to find the prisoners quickly, free them and escape. Captain Sheffield was a fool, or had been a fool, depending on whether or not he was still alive. In any case, the man's career was finished and with his, probably his own. Success with this task was his only hope to salvage his career.

He felt weary in body and soul. The meaningless wandering seemed for naught so he decided to return to the house and have his supper. Tomorrow, he told himself, may be more fruitful.

They had caught a dozen fish, none large enough for a meal but together enough for a stew. Donland entered the house to the smell of the stew cooking. It increased his hunger two-fold, as did his thirst. He lifted the jug of water and drank. It was then he noticed the stew pot over the fire. "A new addition to the household?" he asked.

"Aye, Mister Dobbs appropriated it along with some carrots and onions." Honest answered.

"He stole it?"

"Aye, I would stake money on it."

Donland was curious so he asked, "Did you not question his intentions before he left to steal the pot?"

"that I did and his answer was that he was going to take care of some personal business. When he returned he had the pot and vegetables."

Donland sighed and replied, "I shall have a word with him. This place hangs thieves outright. I'd not care to see him hanging from a gibbet for stealing a pot. Where is he?"

"He and Williamson set out to buy more wine, seems they've the coin you gave them."

Donland doubted that very much. If anything, they were off to steal more wine. Should they be caught he'd not intervene. "Let them hang!" he said as much to himself as he did Honest.

"That would not do, sir! Either of those two would tell about you to save their necks then we'd all be set for the noose."

Honest's words caught him off guard, he was correct. "I shall see where they are about, Where's David and Simon?"

"I sent them to fetch more wood," Honest answered while stirring the pot.

"Keep them here until I return," Donland said as he slammed his hat on his head.

"Aye," Honest said to Donland's back.

Dobbs and Williamson were coming towards him as he gained the street. Each man carried a bottle and a jug.

"Wine?" Donland asked.

"Aye, wine and rum," Dobbs answered.

"Stolen?" Donland asked.

"No, we bought it?"

Donland turned and entered the house. Dobbs and Williamson followed and set the bottles and jugs on the table. They were giddy and at least a sheet if not two to the wind.

Donland came around the table between the two and picked up both jugs then smashed them together. Shards of clay flew in all directions. He faced them and said, "No grog! And there better damn well be no more stealing. All our necks are on the block and you best remember it. Those that rule here have no laws and they hang whom they please. There'll be no solicitor to appeal your case."

"But sir!" Williamson began to plead.

In a flash, Donland pulled his sword and held the tip within an inch of Williamson's neck. There was no mistake in his anger when he said, "It is a question of my neck and I can assure you that I will slit your throat before I have it put in a noose. Do not tempt me for I'll have no mercy!"

Dobbs reached out and grasped Williamson's arm, he said softly, "Andy don't play the fool."

Williamson managed, "Beg pardon, sir, I'll mind my p's and q's."

"See that you do, both of you. As I said, these that rule here have no mercy. You best understand that betraying me will not put you in graces with them. I've seen their kind kill their own to save their own necks. They'll not trust you even if you do them a kindness. You're nothing to them. If you are intent on living, you best continue with me, for if you remain here, sooner or later your life will be forfeit. A word will slip and they will know that you were in *Brune's* company."

"Aye," Dobbs answered. Williamson swallowed.

Donland lowered his sword.

"The stew is ready!" Honest announced.

Donland turned, slipping his sword back into the scabbard as he did so.

Honest held out a crude clay cup. "Simon found these behind the house. They're not stole!"

Donland took the cup. The fish stew was hot, almost as hot as his tempter. He settled as he swallowed. He thought on how precarious their situation was. Were he at sea, he could manage gale or shot but here on land without friend and only foes, he was totally on his own. He had no ship's officers and company to lend aide or advice. There were only these few and two of which he was having difficulty trusting. Between them they had scarce a few pennies. The situation was compounded by the knowledge that his career and livelihood depended on successfully rescuing the prisoner.

"Another cup?" Honest asked dragging Donland from his thoughts.

He faked a smile and say, "aye."

The house was too hot so Donland stepped outside into the cooling night air. David followed him. Neither spoke until Donland had settled himself on the crude log bench. David asked, "Sir, what became of the man?"

Donland had known the question would come. He answered, "He gave me no choice, there's no need to ask more." It wasn't a lie but not the truth either. He did not wish David to think ill of him.

"I thought it would come to that. He would have tried you, he was that sort."

"Aye," Donland answered and asked, "What of your day?"

David seemed glad of the change in conversation. He answered, "We fished, I caught nothing but Simon caught the biggest one. Honest and Williamson would occasional start conversations with those who passed. Dobbs slept a great deal. It was, I guess, a lonely day. My mind wandered to days aboard *Hornet*, I miss her."

"And I," Donland confessed. He did not add that he missed *Hornet* more than he had ever missed anything or anyone. At times he thought he missed Betty Sumerford so much that he considered resigning his commission and going to her but then reason and obligation prevailed.

Still, on moonlit nights with warm breezes he would let his mind drift to the island, to walks at sunset with her. Remembering the first time their lips had met would cause his heart to beat a little faster and his pulse would race. In his dreams she would hold him and whisper sweet words of love just as she had done for real in Charles Town. Yes, he longed for her but not in the same way he longed to have *Hornet*.

Chapter Seven

Jackson sat with his eyes closed and his back propped against a tree. He was trying to visualize a map in his head. The island they were on could be anyone of six, he had not a clue to which one they had washed ashore on.

"Boat there!" Scott said and pointed.

Jackson sat up at once and turned in the direction Scott pointed. The boat was only a fisherman, nothing of consequence. He said to Scott, "At least we know there are people about and a village nearby. I suggest we walk along the beach from the direction he came. He'll not have come far."

"Aye," Scott answered and they began to walk. O'Rouke followed several steps behind.

"Have you coin?" Jackson asked his companions.

Scott laughed. "Bloody buggers even took me knife."

They walked on without speaking and soon saw smoke rising just inland from the beach.

Jackson said, "There'll be food."

Neither of the two men answered him. They trudged on and soon came upon two boats lying on the beach with men readying them to go fishing. The men were dark skinned islanders but wore loose trousers. They stopped their labors and watched Jackson and the other two men approach.

"Good day," Jackson greeted and asked, "We be ship-wrecked and adrift, what island is this?"

"St Croix!" The short man with bad teeth answered.

"How far to the nearest town?" Jackson asked

"Christiansted, that way, half day walk!" the man answered and resumed his work.

Jackson turned to the two men with him, "You heard, that's where I'm bound."

Scott said, "I'll have some food first even if I have to steal it."

"Aye," O'Rouke agreed.

Jackson grinned at them and said, "No need for theft, I've a bit of coin the bastards missed. We'll eat and be on our way."

A woman in the first hut they came to gave them beans wrapped in a piece of tough bread and all the water they wanted. She told them where the spring was and suggested they bathe. Jackson agreed, after sweltering in the hot sun for a day and the night on the beach they each stank like week-old fish.

"How much money have you?" Scott asked.

"Never you mind, not enough worth dying for," Jackson answered. He added, "You've wages owed and I've business dealings with a man here who will make me a loan. You'll be paid all you're owed."

Scott did not answer. O'Rouke was likewise silent.

Their silence made Jackson uneasy. He had thought he could trust the two but now he wasn't sure. If they thought he carried money they could pose a risk. Perhaps when they reached the town he would give them a guinea each, it would be more than they were owed and enough to satisfy them for a time.

Christiansted was a fair-sized town. They arrived well before sunset and were hungry. Jackson passed the white gleaming Government House and entered a modest building with large windows. It sat across the street from Government House and on a corner of the square. John Hamilton, the proprietor, in Jackson's estimation was a fair man and not one to waste or sell on the cheap. Likewise, he bargained for what he bought. Tough-minded, he might be but Jackson still counted him a friend.

"You two wait here and I will return with what's owed you, say two guineas?"

Both men's eyes lit up, "Aye, that will do us," O'Rouke exclaimed.

"Mister Jackson, so good to see you but I am surprised," Hamilton said when Jackson was shown into his office. Hamilton was a large man in girth and height with curly black hair tied in a que.

"Aye, I'm a bit surprised to be here today as well. My ship was taken and the crew set me adrift. I've nothing but what you see."

Hamilton looked Jackson up and down, "That explains questions I had, I'd doubted what I was told and am relieved to see you."

"Questions, Mister Hamilton?" Jackson asked.

Hamilton smiled a half-smile and answered, "A man by the name of Owens came here, said you had died and he was now *Folly*'s master. Wanted to sell not only what was in the hold but the ship as well. I confess that I did purchase the cargo but not the ship, I had no need of it."

"Fair price for the cargo?" Jackson asked.

"Half the value," Hamilton answered and continued, "I made an offer and he accepted, that was when I became suspicious. Now, I could have purchased the ship but I was dubious about the circumstances. You understand?"

"I do and I find no fault in your purchasing the cargo, it is of no importance the way things have played out. I do, however, ask a favor?"

"A loan?" Hamilton asked.

"Aye, a small one just to tide me over until I recover *Folly*."

"That you may have and no interest, let us call it a courtesy. How much will you require?"

"Ten pounds will be sufficient. I have four times that on deposit in Savannah," Jackson answered.

"I've no doubt of that," Hamilton said then reached into his coat and brought out his wallet. Without hesitation he extracted twenty pounds in five-pound notes. "I'm certain of the repayment, and once you have regained your property we shall again do business and I shall prosper by it."

"No interest?" Jackson asked.

"None," Hamilton answered.

Jackson took the money and said, "I am in your debt far more than the sum."

Hamilton smiled and said, "You are a man I can trust and a man to whom I could go if I were in need. The debt for now is yours but a turn of fortune could have me at your door. Let's us prosper if God allows."

"Aye," Jackson answered. He asked, "May I have your clerk exchange a note for coin? I've men outside to be paid off."

"With my blessings," Hamilton answered. His countenance changed as if something had just occurred to him and he said, "I know where *Folly* is bound?"

Jackson exclaimed, "That I would know!"

Hamilton answered, "Town of Luquillo on the island of Puerto Rico. Owens asked me where he might sell the ship and I told him a man by the name of Morrison deals in such vessels."

"I know the place well, I'd have paid all I have to know where Owens was bound and when. I will have the bugger's heart out of him and use it for fish bait!"

Hamilton again smiled, "Just do the deed at Luquillo, pirates have no law against such."

55

"Aye," Jackson answered and extended his hand in thanks.

Donland rose early, ate a few crusts of bread and downed the remainder of a bottle of wine. It was a poor breakfast and if the day proceeded as it had begun there would be no supper for any of them. Honest stirred and sat up. Dobbs was snoring loudly but the others did not notice.

"Off are you?" Honest asked.

"Aye, to the shops and to see who is about," Donland answered. "I will return in an hour or so, keep them here until I return."

"Aye," Honest answered.

Tradesmen and fishermen were about. Some were entering café's for their breakfast. One man dressed as a merchant neared and Donland decided to engage him in conversation. "Morning sir, have you a moment?"

The man looked up and down at Donland and stopped. "A moment only," the man replied.

"I'm seeking a Mister Morrison, would you know his home?"

"Morrison lives a street over but he'll not see you there, he'll be in his office in an hour just there," the man said and pointed.

"Thank you for your kindness," Donland answered and tipped his hat.

Donland continued down the street and saw the sign hanging over the door announcing it as "Morrison Company." He walked by and on to the beach. He would return in an hour.

A goodly breeze was blowing so he walked with it blowing into his face. There was a sail, he stopped and watched as it drew near. To his amazement he recognized her; it was *Folly*. She remained under sail, cruising close inshore. He stood still and watched as her sails were furled and her anchor dropped. He smiled to himself as he thought of Jackson coming ashore and of sharing a pint together. They would have tales to tell.

The hour was passed and those in the house would be waiting his return but he lingered. A boat was put over the *Folly*'s side he would wait for Jackson before returning to the house.

He moved along the beach until he came to the chandler's shop and sat down in the shade cast by the building. The boat began to pull for the shore and Donland's keen sight told him that Jackson was not in the boat. He waited and watched as the boat was beached and six men came ashore. There were none that were familiar to him. A wiry man with red hair and chops seemed to be in charge and there was little doubt that he was angry.

The men separated once they were on the street. Four went into a saloon and the redhead and a tall heavy-built man continued in the direction of the center of town. Donland followed at a distance. The men entered the building Donland had just left. He was curious as to what business the red-haired man would have with the proprietor.

"Interesting," Donland said to himself. He decided to wait and once the redhead left he would follow. Whatever business the redhead was conducting would not be with Jackson's consent.

Curiosity got the better of him so he crossed the street and walked to the Morrison Company. He paused in front of the window for a moment as if examining his reflection then moved on. To his surprise, in that one moment, the redhead shook hands with a well tailored man, most likely Morrison.

The redhead and the other man left the building and headed toward the saloon where the four men had entered earlier. Donland quickened his pace slightly and followed. He entered the establishment as the redhead was sitting down; the man was beaming and seemed overjoyed.

The saloon was a low ceiling room and contained six tables and a bar. Donland purposely passed close to the table were the redhead sat. He heard the redhead say, "he'll buy her". Then all six men shouted "huzza!" and slapped one other on the shoulder. Two raised their glasses as if toasting some deed. Donland knew exactly what they were talking about; they were selling Jackson's *Folly*. But "where was Jackson?" that was his question and how had these men gained possession of her. It mattered not; he knew what he must do.

Chapter Eight

Honest and the others were in the house fuming about the lack of food and wondering where Donland was. Dobbs said, "It's been mor'n an hour. Nigh on two!"

Donland entered and interrupted them with, "We've no time to waste, there's an anchored ship for the taking. There's no more than two aboard keeping watch. If we are to leave this place then we must be quick about taking her before others of her crew return. Grab whatever weapons you have and follow me!"

He turned for the door and ran down the street. Only once did he glance back to make sure they were following. Honest was in the rear of the group and he was certain there had been threats.

A few heads turned as Donland ran past and he grinned, they would think the group of men behind him were giving chase.

The boat was where those from the *Folly* had left her. No doubt they were still in the saloon celebrating their good fortune. That was good for Donland wanted no fight. He could not risk even one man being injured, he needed each one if he were to sail *Folly* away from Luquillo.

Simon and David arrived before Honest and the other two men. Donland ordered, "Push her out!"

They obeyed and with a great heave started the boat into the surf. Dobbs and Williamson arrived and they too shoved. When Honest arrived, Donland ordered, "Take up oars!" He bellied over the gunnel and took an oar, the others likewise took oars and in an instant turned the boat. They were away and there was no pursuit. "Now!" Donland shouted as a wave curled in front of the boat. "Pull!" He ordered and the boat shot through the crest.

Once in the trough he placed his oar in the bottom of the boat and seated himself in the rear. He announced, "I must appear as the new owner, take no heed to my words. We'll take her once we are aboard. Show no mercy, pistols or knives it matters not but it must be quickly done. Once done, we set all sail, Mister Welles you will have the helm!"

"Aye," David answered and pulled on the oar in rhythm with the others.

Two men stood amidships watching the boat approach. Donland was aware of their eyes and his mind was reeling as to what he would say. Somehow he had to convince them to let him board. He decided not to use his original ruse of perspective owner, his clothes were too shabby. He considered being a pirate coming to buy but abandoned that thought. Finally he decided to be an agent of Morrison Company and was to inspect the boat. It was a more suitable lie and what he wore was more appropriate to that role.

"What's your purpose?" A scruffy man with a torn shirt and a mop of brown hair called.

Donland answered, "Morrison Company, your redheaded man is making a deal for the vessel, I'm sent to inspect it!"

The man consulted the red-beefy man with no shirt. Donland took the opportunity to whisper to Honest, "When you hear me take him, shoot the other one!"

"Aye," Honest whispered back and added, "I'll pass the word in case I miss my mark."

"Come aboard, leave your pistol and sword! Only you, the others best stay put if they value breathing!" the man called down.

Donland had not expected that from the man. "Slip your knife into my boot," Donland whispered to Honest as he stood and unbuckled his sword.

Honest obeyed and slid the knife into the Donland's boot as Donland stepped across the gunnel to the rung of the ladder. The two men above did not notice.

Donland smiled as he gained the deck. He glanced up and down the deck to make sure there were no others hiding.

"Ramsey send you?" the man asked while pointing his pistol at Donland.

"No, Mister Morrison, I work for him," Donland answered. He walked forward and appeared to be assessing the sail and rigging. "Rigging looks worn," he mused loudly.

The man followed leaving the other man watching over the boat.

"Have you cargo?" Donland asked.

"No cargo, just the ship. She's a good sailor," the man said as Donland examined the bow.

"So you say, so you say." Donland said as he peered over the gunnel. "I'll have a look below now."

"What's that about?" the beefy man questioned loud enough for his mate to hear and pointed to men on the beach. The man with Donland turned slightly to see what was occurring on the beach. It was the last thing he did on this earth, Donland plucked the knife from his boot and plunged the blade into the man's belly. The man's face displayed first shock and then horror as his eyes went to the blade. Before the dying man hit the deck two pistols fired. The other man went down with a ball in his head and one in his chest.

Donland wasted no time and jerked the axe that was kept next to the anchor cable. With two blows he severed the cable.

"See to the aft anchor!" Donland yelled to Honest.

"Dobbs you and Williamson to the foremast and loose the main!" Once done, come down and help with the buntlines and clews!"

"Anchor catted!" Honest shouted from aft.

With the cable cut and nothing to hold *Folly*, the wind pushed against her hull with enough force to cause her to begin to drift westward. Donland pulled the pins on the larboard side to free the buntlines and hurriedly loosed the clews.

He shouted to Simon who was on the port side, "Buntline pins and clews!"

The boy followed Donland's lead. Together they pulled to stabilize the yard as Dobbs and Williamson loosed the sail.

Honest hurried to Simon and began to pull. "Take up the buntlines!" he ordered his son.

"Lend a hand!" Donland shouted to the two men on the mast.

"I've steerage!" David shouted.

With the help of Dobbs and Williamson, the sail came round and filled. Each man began securing lines.

"That will be enough to keep us from the beach! Back up you go lads!" Donland ordered Dobbs and Williamson.

Each of them knew they were too few to work the ship, it required two watches of at least eight each. Were they to be pursued they would not evade the pursuers. They would need luck to do more.

"Topsail clews and bunts!" Donland shouted to Honest as he pulled the pins on his side of the ship.

Once again Dobbs and Williamson unlashed the sail and then returned to the deck to help with the lines.

"Steer north by west!" Donland shouted to David.

By Donland's estimate they were making just over two knots.

Honest crossed the deck to Donland and asked. "We've got her now what shall we do with her?"

Donland had asked himself the same question and answered, "First, I will go below and see if there is anyone about."

"Mister Jackson?" Honest asked.

"Aye, he is either a prisoner below or dead. Manage best you can here until I return."

He made his way to the hatch and went below. The cabin door was ajar and he found what he thought he would find. The cabin was ransacked and empty bottles and jugs lay strewn about. There was nothing to indicate anyone else was aboard. It appeared to him that the eight men had taken the ship and either killed Jackson or stolen the ship while she was in port. There was no evidence of bloodletting in the cabin, which meant there was a good chance Jackson was alive. Nevertheless, *Folly* was his for the moment.

Donland retraced his steps and went on deck. David was still at the wheel. Dobbs, Williamson and Honest tended the sails. He scanned the horizon and saw no ships.

"David continue to steer north by west. We should be able to clear the next headland without difficulty and I do not expect the battery to fire on us. Once we are out of sight of the land we will lie-to and wait for more favorable winds so that we may sail east."

"Aye, Captain," David replied with a huge grin.

"Three pounds and not a penny less," the owner of the small schooner was adamant.

Jackson knew the man was correct and were he in his shoes he'd not do it for less. "Aye, three then," he agreed.

It was expensive but sailing into a pirate's lair was precarious. Adophus Bingham was a cautious man but he liked money and he gladly took Jackson's. Hamilton had said that Bingham could be trusted and that was worth something, probably more than money. He only hoped *Folly* would be anchored and the three of them could steal her back. O'Rouke and Scott were willing to try for a price.

They sailed on the tide shortly after sunrise and by Bingham's estimate, provided the wind stayed fair, would arrive by nightfall. That suited Jackson, for once landed he would have the night to formulate a plan for re-taking *Folly*. Having retaken her, if Owens still lived he would hang from the yardarm before the sun set. There was no one in Luquillo to object and if anyone did, well they would have to chase *Folly* to the ends of the earth.

The bell aboard Bingham's *Belle Rose* struck three times in the first dogwatch. Jackson checked his watch and saw that it was just after five. He was impatient but there was nothing he could do, it wasn't his ship.

"She's over the horizon," Jackson said to Bingham who stood at the wheel.

"Aye, that she be but since I'm this far north I may as well run south down to Luquillo. Them guns on the eastern headlands have been known to practice at anything that sails by. Drunks and fools they be, just firing for sport."

There was no need to argue with the man, they would still reach Luquillo before sunset. He turned and walked the length of the deck to the bow. The flat green sea was empty; the glare intense so he shaded his eyes. He stood there for several minutes squinting against the glare, waiting for *Belle Rose* to tack and run south.

He was about to turn away when he thought he saw a mast. Standing there with the wind to his back he shaded his eyes again with his hand and stared, she was there, only a mast directly ahead. Bingham had not seen it.

Jackson kept his eye on the mast and watched it grow. He saw she was a ship-rigged with two masts. This close to Luquillo she would be either a privateer or a trader. He decided to have a look and turned about to fetch a glass. Before he was even amidships, Bingham pulled a glass from the rack and put it to his eye.

"Prepare to go about!" Bingham shouted to his small crew.

Jackson ignored the call and reached for the glass and put it to his eye. What he saw surprised him and in the same instant made his blood boil. It was *Folly*!

"Belay Bingham, she's *Folly*!" Jackson shouted.

"Mor'n likely taken by some pirate, best to avoid her."

Jackson was anxious, "Ten pounds, I'll give you ten pounds more to run down to her!"

Bingham's eyes widened, "ten pounds you say?"

"Aye, and I have it on me," Jackson stated.

Bingham considered for a moment and said, "I'll close with her but not in gun range and set you off in a boat for five pounds, I'll do no more!"

"That will not benefit me, close with her and if she fires a shot then you can go about. By then I will be able to see who is aboard, you'll get the ten pounds either way."

"Devil of a risk!" Bingham said.

"Aye, but ten pounds for your purse," Jackson said.

"I'll go no closer than a gun can shoot," Bingham agreed.

"Aye!" Jackson said with glee and added, "I will go below and fetch O'Rouke and Scott.

"You sure?" O'Rouke asked.

"Aye, it be *Folly* right enough," Jackson answered.

"I've a score to settle, left me for dead he did. I'll have his liver for my supper," Scott stated.

"You're welcome to it!" Jackson said and turned back for the hatch. The two men followed him up. Scott asked as they reached the deck, "Have you pistols and swords, I'd no go aboard without both?"

Jackson didn't turn to answer but said over his shoulder, "Nor I, you'll have both."

Bingham was still at the helm and Jackson said to him, "We'll need weapons."

"Aye, perhaps we all will if the wind veers, but I've plenty aboard," Bingham replied.

Folly was lying-to with her bow pointing east and there was activity on her deck. Jackson could make out only four men trying to manage the sails. He wondered where the others were. He reasoned that there should be eight men, it would take at least that to manage *Folly*.

"Only six aboard her!" Jackson shouted to Bingham. It would ease Bingham's mind to know there was no threat to his ship.

"You said she carried six-pounders. It'll take at least six men just to load, train and fire one of those and there'd be none to mind the sails or helm," Bingham mused.

Jackson lifted his glass and studied the man standing midships trying to haul the sail around. Another figure came into view. He almost shouted the boy's name, David!

"Close with her Captain Bingham, she's in good hands. Captain Donland has her!" Jackson shouted.

"Who the blazes is he?" Bingham asked as Jackson crossed the deck.

"Navy, Captain of *Hornet*, he was my captain. He's cut her out by God!"

"Are you certain?" Bingham asked.

"Aye, as certain as you are going to get your ten pounds!" Jackson said. He was beside himself.

Folly's foremast sails were filling and spilling wind but she was beginning to move, trying to go about.

"No steerage!" David called.

Donland knew in his heart that it was hopeless. They were too few to manage getting *Folly* to go about and get away. His best hope was to surrender if the oncoming ship was a pirate. In his heart he prayed she was just a merchantman, another island trader that recognized *Folly* and was coming to lend aid.

He looked up and saw a man standing in the bows with a glass in his hand. The man would be able to see him clearly at this distance. Something about the man's stance seemed familiar. He could only hope.

The man in the bow lowered his glass and shouted, "Ahoy! *Folly*!" The hail was a total shock. It came again and Donland answered, "*Hornet*!"

Chapter Nine

After receiving the ten pounds, Bingham put a boat over the side and sent four of his men to crew it. Donland watched, as did the others as the boat closed with *Folly*. He could not resist a smile upon seeing his friend sitting in the boat.

Jackson came over the side followed by Scott and O'Rouke. Donland greeted Jackson with a handshake but Jackson brushed it aside and bear-hugged him. Donland returned the gesture.

"I feared you dead," Donland said as he faced his old friend.

"Aye, they tried but like O'Rouke said, "I was too damn mad to die."

Donland laughed, the traces of anger were evident in Jackson's voice.

"Then we shall have to settle the score," Donland said.

Jackson nodded and said, "Aye, that will come but what of you? How have you come to have *Folly*?"

"A tale to be told over rum, there is still some below. Your mates consumed most of it."

"I've a taste for a drop," Jackson answered and turned to Scott, "Take in the sail and put the gaskets on then all of you come below!"

"Aye, Captain!" Scott answered.

Jackson picked up two mugs lying on the deck and set them on the table. Donland found the partial jug of rum and poured. He began, "*Hornet* was sold to the Americans and I was ordered to *Brune* to lead a party to Luquillo since I've knowledge of the place."

"You're to be paid off and thrown on the beach after that," Jackson stated matter of fact.

"Aye," Donland answered after swallowing a sip of rum. "They'll not need me after this. Captain Sheffield refused sound advice and lost his ship. It went aground on the banks near the eastern battery and blew up. I doubt there were any survivors. I and those with me were already on shore so we were spared. But when the accounting is done, I will be the one held accountable. My only hope of redemption will be to complete the task which we were about."

"Prisoners, I would suspect, there be little else to concern the admirals." Jackson stated.

Donland held the mug but did not drink. "One I'm not allowed to name, not even to those who assist me."

Jackson lifted his mug, set it down and studied Donland. "You'll need a ship to get you back there and to take you off."

"Aye," Donland agreed.

Their eyes met and Jackson said, "*Folly* is yours to do with as you will. I can't speak for Scott and O'Rouke but I am yours to command. I owe you as much for getting *Folly* back under my heels."

Donland reached across the table and grasped Jackson forearm; "I had time to consider how to proceed while we lay-to and concluded it would be best to sail to Fajardo. From there I will go overland as before and attempt the rescue. If *Folly* were to remain on station there to receive us when we return it would be of great help. I can't and won't ask more of you that that."

"Once you return, then I shall deal with that bastard Owens!" Jackson said and lifted his mug.

Donland smiled, "Aye, justice! But before that I've to accomplish the task. We've men enough to sail and you'll have enough remaining to lay-to and wait."

Jackson reached for the jug. The clatter from the hatch announced that the others were coming down.

"I trust there remains enough for them to have their ration," Donland said.

Jackson rose from the chair as Honest entered followed by Dobbs. "Find yourself a mug or tankard, there be some lying about," Jackson said as he lifted the lid of a chest. He reached in and produced another jug and then removed a false bottom. He brought out a purse and opened it, "Aye, the bastards found the rum and were satisfied to look no further. I've the money for another crew, I should be able to gain some hands in Fajardo."

He smiled and said, "Here lads, drink your fill for we will lay-to for the night, at first light we set sail."

Honest was in the bow with the lead. With each cast he called out the dept. "By the mark deep three!"

"We've water to spare," Jackson said. "Our draft is no more than twelve feet, and this is the most shallow part of the channel. I remember it well from before."

"Aye," Donland answered.

"Can you find your way across?" Jackson asked.

Donland thought for a moment and answered, "We followed a narrow track when we landed but it soon joined a larger one which I believe originated in the town. This time we will begin in the town, I'm not concerned about encountering any Spanish troops. The way to Luquillo should be well traveled and easily discerned."

"How long do you think it will take you to find your man and return?" Jackson asked.

"By the mark three and half!" Honest sang out.

Donland was glad of the call, it gave him a moment to formulate his answer. "If I am correct and the prisoner I'm seeking is where I believe him to be then, we should return in less than three days. The other prisoners are possibly held somewhere else but they are not my concern. If I can retrieve the one I seek without difficulty then, as I said, we will be on the beach in three days or less."

"I would come with you but I fear I'd be of little value, I've not wind for such travel anymore."

Donland nodded and asked, "The wound still troubles you?"

"Aye," Jackson answered and added, "But as master of my own ship, I do as I please. With a good first mate, I seldom do more than the occasional watch. It's easy enough for me and I want for nothing more than a night in port with a woman."

"Always the woman," Donland mocked.

"Aye, and what of Betty Sumerford?" Jackson asked.

"I've a letter from time to time and she is to return to Charles Town next month and I wish to see her. If I'm cast onto the beach, I can do as you, as I please when I please," Donland said and grinned.

"Aye you could and no man would fault you for it. You've proven your courage more than once. And, if any man question it I'll take him to task."

Donland laughed.

"Just so you know, it's no longer Charles Town it was changed to Charleston. I'd not want you to appear the fool," Jackson said and grinned.

"Sail!" Dobbs called down from the mast.

"Where away?" Jackson called up.

"Port bow!" Dobbs answered,

"Seems we will have company in Fajardo. I will go up and see if she is a man of war," Donland said and rose.

"Aye," Jackson agreed.

Donland Climbed the shrouds and when he was even with the yard, turned and focused the telescope on the small ship He called down, "Island schooner!" He studied her for a few seconds then began the climb down.

Jackson asked as Donland gained the deck," See her flag?"

"Aye, an American."

"The *Lady Ash*, out of Charleston, Hugo Benson is her master and owner. Bastard of a man, he'll steal a cargo off the docks if he can."

"You speak as if you know him."

"I know him right enough, right after I got *Folly* he stole cargo from me. It was in the warehouse waiting for me. He showed up with a fake bill of laden and took it. But I got even, he was stuck fast in the mud, the only way to free *Lady Ash* was to unload cargo onto *Folly*. When *Lady Ash* came off he got half the cargo back. He swore to kill me and take *Folly* but he's not been able to do either."

"Will he interfere?"

"If he thinks it will hurt me, he would find a way. But, I'll not give him an opportunity."

Jackson stayed aboard *Folly* as Donland and the others rowed ashore. Scott and O'Rouke would beach the boat and go in search of men to join the crew. Jackson had determined to make Scott first mate and thereby bind him to the ship. He had proved himself reliable enough and by giving him a position he reasoned Scott would be trustworthy. O'Rouke, although, more stable and less hotheaded would have been the better choice but he needed both men. Today would test Scott's mettle, as he was to secure men for the crew, men he could trust, as he was now first mate.

Donland climbed from the boat first and was followed by the others. Each was armed with a pistol and either a knife or a sword. They parted company with Scott and O'Rouke upon reaching the street.

It was midday and the sun was bearing down. Sweat beaded and rolled down Donland's face as he hurriedly led the men through the town. Fortunately, they did not encounter any Spanish soldiers or anyone to challenge them. It was in his mind to reach Luquillo as quickly as possible and return with as much haste as possible. There sooner he was back aboard *Folly* and sailing for Antigua, the better.

He passed what he guessed to be the last house of the town when a voice shouted, "Donland!"

He stopped and turned to see who had called his name. To his complete surprise a man wearing a uniform coat was jogging toward him. As he drew near, Donland recognized him, Lieutenant Carstairs!

"Gawd, I never thought I'd see you again!" Carstairs exclaimed.

"Nor, I you," Donland remarked. "I thought the sharks or the pirates had you."

"Neither, although we had to swim for it. Managed to turn one of the boats back over and make it to shore. We walked for days through jungle and swamps to reach this place. I thought the Spaniards would aid us but they only laughed at my plight. What of you?"

"We're about the mission to rescue the prisoner," Donland answered.

"Surely not now, not with *Brune* lost!"

Donland did not answer but asked, "How many have you?"

Carstairs' face reflected his confusion but he managed, "Seven, four marines and three seamen."

"Get them and be quick about it. We've not time to dally."

"I'll not!" Carstairs blurted.

Donland had no time for foolish quivering, "Either you will fetch them or I shall have you brought up on charges for disobeying a superior's orders and shirking your duty."

Carstairs' face went white with realization but his belligerence remained. "You are not my superior and you'll not live to say anything if you go back there. You've not men enough to succeed!"

"Damn your eyes man! I know where our man is and it is only a matter of effort to bring him out and I have a ship waiting to take us from here. If you have any sense remaining in your head you will obey my order and fetch those men."

Donland turned, "Mister Welles you and Honest go with Lieutenant Carstairs and bring the men!"

"Aye, Captain!" David answered.

Carstairs made to continue to object but when Honest took him by the arm and turned him about he said nothing.

Carstairs and Honest returned in a quarter of an hour with six men.

Donland asked, "I thought you said seven?"

"One has gone missing, a marine named of Femster, a troublemaker and will not be missed," Carstairs snarled.

"Then we will be off Mister Carstairs. Walk with me," Donland said "It's just over a two hour walk, we'll have time to sort things out."

"Aye," Carstairs answered grudgingly.

Donland noticed the young man kept one shoulder drooping and asked, "Did you escape uninjured?"

"Splinters in my shoulder. Hurts like the blazes. Corporal Jones removed them and strapped my wounds. The worst part was the rum he poured into the wounds, gawd it burned!"

"Your first time to be wounded?" Donland asked as he ducked under a low branch.

Sheepishly Carstairs answered, "Aye."

"Sir, how many times have you been wounded?" David asked.

Donland let the question hang before answering. "I'd not know and I don't think about the wounds, only that I lived. God is merciful and that's no error."

"Aye," Carstairs agreed. "Good men died and better men than myself perished when *Brune* exploded. Were it not for that blast of grape showering me with splinters, I'd been standing and killed. I've had time to think about it and concluded that at the moment of my wounding that it was the worst thing that has

74

ever occurred in my life but then I realize it was what saved my life. Odd isn't it?"

Donland replied, "Odd, no, it is just a matter of how events unfold. No man can know what the next hour brings and if he thought he did then he would be miserable beyond redemption. It is the roll of the dice, sometimes sixes, sometimes ones. You can't know and you can't cheat death. It is the way of things."

They walked on in silence, each man locked in his own thoughts. Men cursed the persistent buzzing and biting of mosquitoes and gnats. Almost every man tied a rag around his forehead to stop the sweat from running into his eyes. The heat was draining them and after the first hour Donland called a halt near a stream.

The men lay on their bellies and drank their fill and then fell back and rested. Those that had bread in their pockets ate; others sought wild fruit. Donland had neither and contented himself with the water. Carstairs sat cradling his wounded shoulder.

"Does it pain you?" Donland asked.

"Aye, but more than that is the itch that is driving me mad. I dare not scratch for fear of making it worse."

Donland was sympathetic for he had suffered similar wounds and knew of the ongoing torment. "Aye, best to avoid scratching for it does only make it worse. In another day it will become tolerable."

"Have you a plan for when we reach Luquillo?" the young man asked.

Donland considered his answer before speaking; it was as good a time as any to tell him what was expected. "There is a man that goes by the name Morrison, he owns a trading company and I suspect ships. I would also wager that he is a pirate. A high wall surrounds his house and he has guards posted at the gate. It is my intention to go over the wall at night in hopes of finding the prisoner we are tasked to retrieve. I feel certain he is there but I've no proof."

"And what of us?" Carstairs asked.

"If I am successful locating the prisoners then I will prepare the way for our party to enter. You will lead the men and take the guards and any others that oppose you. All must be done with knives and swords and with as little noise as possible. We raise alarm at our own peril. Then we will be away as swiftly as possible before help can be summoned."

"They will pursue us!" Carstairs stated.

"Aye, and probably with horses. Which means that it will be a running fight."

"But sir, against odds and so lightly armed, what hope have we?"

Donland had considered the pursuit and he answered, "There should be arms available in the house so we must take all that we can carry. From time to time we will delay our pursuit by ambushing our pursuers. We have no other course open to us."

Carstairs' face showed his skepticism.

Donland pursed his lips then explained, "My career and your career hang in the balance. If we are not successful in this venture we will both be held accountable for not just the failure but for the loss of *Brune*. Those above us must have someone on which to place blame. As we are the only two officers remaining, it falls upon us."

"Perhaps you more so than I," Carstairs said with indignation.

The retort that came into Donland's mind was strangled before it got to his tongue. "Perhaps, but do not forget that Captain Sheffield placed you in command of the task ashore."

Carstairs said nothing. He rose and strode to the stream.

"The little bastard would have you hanged," Honest whispered.

Donland turned, he had not been aware of Honest's nearness. "Aye, he would but he'll not have the opportunity. A man can fail many times but death comes but once."

"I'll be going over the wall with you," Honest said.

"No, I'll take Dobbs. I will need you to insure Mister Carstairs doesn't foul the plan. Should he make the attempt he must be silenced, not killed just silenced."

76

Honest grinned, "Aye, silenced in a way he'd not know what hit him. The lads would look the other way and testify so if needed."

Chapter Ten

They came within a hundred yards of the edge of the town and Donland veered off into the jungle. His intention was to return to the house in which they had stayed and wait there until dark. Halfway to the house they began to smell a terrible stench. Donland knew at once the source of the smell and avoided the site. David did not need that memory nor did he need to suspect what had occurred.

The house was undisturbed and they entered in late afternoon. He began giving orders. "Sweet and Emery fetch us some wood. Honest collect what food we have and prepare a meal. The rest of you clean and check your weapons. We will wait until full on dark before proceeding."

"Mister Carstairs shed your coat, your shirt will sufficient for the evening. We will walk around Morrison's house."

"Mister Welles you maintain order here and see no man gets into rum or mischief!"

"Aye, sir," David answered.

Carstairs shed his coat and stuffed a pistol into his belt.

"How is your shoulder?" Donland asked.

"I'll bear up," Carstairs answered.

"We'll avoid those on the street as much as possible," Donland cautioned.

The two men set off. Fires lighted houses, as the evening meals were prepared. A few children played in the street and dogs barked at them as they walked past. Neither Donland nor Carstairs spoke as they went. It was only when they neared the house did Donland say, "Take note of your surroundings. In the dark, you might lose your way and be lost to us."

Carstairs did not speak.

The man's sullenest was irritating Donland. He was glad of the earlier opportunity to speak with Honest. Truth was that he was more confident having Honest watching over the men rather than Carstairs. In his heart he believed that at the first opportunity Carstairs would cut and run.

They walked along the side of the street away from the guards. There was still only two, one or either side of the iron gate. Of the occupants in the house, there was not a sound or a light. Voices and sounds from other houses floated on the breeze. Donland and Carstairs turned the corner, a yapping dog charged at them and made to attack but when Donland turned and walked backwards, the dog proceeded no closer.

"Curr!" Carstairs said with disdain.

Donland ignored the remark.

Once they were well away from the house Donland spoke, "You see the wall, it extends all the way around the property. My guess it is eight feet high so I will require assistance to scale it. The corner we just passed is where I will go over. The tree that hangs over the wall should aid my decent."

"Aye, and have you considered how I will dispatch the guards?"

Donland answered, "I have and will explain what is to be done after we've our supper."

79

Honest was again minding the pot when Donland and Carstairs returned. "Beans and salt pork," Honest said in the way of greeting.

Donland laid his hat on the table and addressed the men. "We'll have our supper and rest. I see no need of making the rescue attempt until near dawn. There are too many about and I rather not risk the road through the jungle at night."

The men gathered about Donland in the faint light of the fire as he took a stick and drew a crude square in the sand. "This," he said, "Is the wall surrounding the house in town. What we are about is the rescue of prisoners, one is especially important to our admiral. Let me caution you, be silent as mice for we have not the men to take on the pirates. The last time I was tasked here to free prisoners the pirates were aided by the Spanish garrison in San Juan. Therefore, we must be silent and swift or we will all be dead by morning."

He had their attention and continued. He drew a small circle in one corner. "This is a tree that I will use to gain entry to the grounds and the house. If I discover the prisoners then I will whistle to signal that I have found them."

He then drew two marks on one side of the square; "Here is the gate into the courtyard that is guarded by two men. The ruse, if necessary, that we will use to gain entry is a fight between the two lads, Mister Welles and Simon. We've used it before to goodly success. Both guards should be distracted for a few moments and when they are, Sweet and Williamson will come from one corner and take one guard while Honest and Corporal Jones will come from the other and take that guard. The rest of you will be led by Mister Carstairs and enter the gate. Knives, swords and bayonets will be used. Firing pistols or muskets will bring down upon us more men than we can contend against. Once the guards are taken, either Dobbs or I will meet you and give you further instructions.

80

Donland paused and looked up into the faces of those gathered around him. "Do your duty and do not hazard your mates! He who plays the fool will answer to me!"

They were somber as Donland stood. "In order not to draw attention we will not leave together but in small groups. Dobbs, Emery and I will leave first. A half-hour after we've gone, Honest, Corporal Jones and Haskins will follow and take a different route. Simon will follow with Sweet, Williamson and Askew. Mister Welles, Lieutenant Carstairs and Smith will follow; Mister Welles knows other route to the house. Mister Carstairs will assemble his party on the east side of the house. If I discover there are no prisoners being held I will climb the wall and signal to return."

He then looked directly at Carstairs. "If this is to be done then it must be quickly done!"

Carstairs said nothing, not even a grunt. Donland trusted the man less and disliked him more. He would be glad of the day they were parted.

"Emery, you and Dobbs give me a leg up," Donland said.

The two obeyed and hefted Donland up and he scrambled onto the wall. It was as he hoped; the tree grew between a small building and the wall. He bent down and whispered, "Up with you Dobbs!"

Emery assisted Dobbs and Donland grasped Dobb's arms and pulled him onto the wall. Once both were settled, Donland reached for a limb of the tree and swung down to the ground without making a sound. Dobbs followed.

There was no light and no sound in the small building, the two crept around to the corner of the building and halted. There was a man just off the veranda leaning against a small tree. Donland decided the man was a guard, a sleepy guard. He ducked back behind the corner and whispered to Dobbs, "Let's try the other corner."

They retraced their steps, rounded the corner and came upon a hedgerow that was chest high. Carefully both men kept low as they moved behind it to its end. Light shone from a window in the main house. The distance to the house from the hedge was about four feet. He peered around the edge of the hedge and saw that the guard was still leaning against the tree and facing away from him.

"Quick as a cat!" he whispered to Dobbs." Then darted to the window. Dobbs followed. He cautiously peeked in, "kitchen," he whispered to Dobbs.

They moved on and came to the corner of the house and to another window, this one without light but with bars on it. Donland could see nothing and he heard no sounds. The next window was the same. Again he listened and heard nothing.

Dobbs nudged Donland and put a finger to his lips. Someone had just come around the corner of the house. They both saw the man and slowly knelt in the shadows. The man was barely visible in the darkness. He lingered for a moment and then disappeared back around the corner.

"Guard?" Dobbs whispered.

"Aye," Donland answered.

Slowly they rose up and began moving along the wall to the next window. Light spilled through the open window and it was also barred. Donland dared a peek and saw a man sitting at a desk. He was an older man perhaps as much as fifty, balding with as much gray as black remaining. His heavy beard was also a mixture of black and gray.

Donland ducked down and whispered, "Morrison! He's an early riser it seems."

The next window they came to was also lighted and when Donland peeked through the bars he saw the same room. It was filled with books and paintings. He could not see the desk from that angle. "Same room," he whispered to Dobbs.

They came to another corner. Donland peeked around and decided that it was the front of the house. There was a large portico with lanterns lighting the entrance. He could not see the wall or the gate and assumed bushes and trees in a garden shielded it. There were no guards so he carefully ventured forth with Dobbs close behind. The first window spilled light into the courtyard. It, as the others, was barred. Donland carefully peeked and saw the same man sitting at the desk, he was still writing.

There were two options, one he could attempt to continue along the front of the house or return the way they had come. He stood still for several long seconds. "I'm going to chance going along the front of the house, you remain here until I return or signal to you."

Dobbs answered, "Aye."

Crouching, Donland edged along the wall of the house. The sand softened his steps. Another window, also barred, shed more light into the courtyard. He peered into it and saw a man walk by and exit by a door, a servant from appearance. The room was furnished with sofas and chairs. Drawing a deep breath and still crouching he came to another window, the room was the one he had just peeked into. Turning, he was able to see the gate but not the guards on the other side of the wall. He crept closer to the portico and the front entrance. A slight breeze rustled the leaves of the trees. He turned toward the gate but saw no one. Cautiously he took two steps and heard a cough from the entrance. He halted and listened; a man cleared his throat and spat. Carefully, he turned about and retraced his steps back to where Dobbs waited. "Another guard at the door," he whispered. "We must go back."

Dobbs followed closely behind Donland as they returned to the rear of the house. The guard had resumed his leaning against the tree and still faced away from them. Overhead, the sky was getting lighter. Whatever he chose to do had to be done soon.

Donland turned to Dobbs and said, "We'll go back along the hedge to the small building. When we get there I'll go around it and wait. You toss a rock or something toward the wall. When the guard turns his back to me, I'll take him."

"Beg pardon, sir, you go and I'll take him, I've done this sort of thing before," Dobbs said.

Donland considered the suggestion. "Don't kill him if you don't have to."

"Aye," Dobbs answered.

Getting to the building and around it was not a problem. Finding stones was. After feeling around in the sand and grass Donland came up with two small seashells. He stood at the corner of the building and flung the first shell as hard as he could in the direction of the wall away from where Dobbs waited. The guard was slow to react, first he pushed away from the trunk of the tree and next he faced the direction the shell had landed. He stood there listening then again leaned against the tree. Donland flung the second shell. This time the guard pulled his pistol and moved quickly toward the wall. Dobbs, barefooted and silent came behind the guard and clubbed him with the butt of his pistol. He managed to catch the man and lower him to the ground. Donland raced over to the two men.

Dobbs looked up, "Ain't killed but I split his head."

"Take his pistol and follow me," Donland said.

"Aye," Dobbs answered and followed.

Donland was careful of his steps on the veranda so as to make no noise. He crossed to the first window and peered in. It was dark except for light from a doorway. He moved on to the next window and found it as the first. The house then extended to his left and he checked three more windows before coming to a corner. He peered around the corner to see another building. A man sat in front of the door.

Donland pulled his watch and tried to see the time but could not. The others would be in position by now and would soon be discovered and the alarm was raised. In another thirty minutes people would begin to stir on the streets as it became light enough to begin their day. If he were to know if there were prisoners in the building he would have to subdue the guard.

"Fetch me the hat and coat of the other guard!" Donland said in Dobbs' ear.

Dobbs slid away as quiet as a cat. Donland remained, gazing again at the sky. Voices caught his attention and he ducked behind the corner. Two men were speaking in Spanish. From the sound of their voices they seemed to be approaching the guard. He knelt and peered around the corner. The guard than had been sitting was standing; he stretched and then spoke to the two men. Donland had to duck back behind the corner when the guard and one man turned back toward the house.

"Sir," Dobbs whispered and held out the hat and coat.

Donland turned, took the coat and hat and put them on. He studied Dobbs for a moment and an idea came to him. "I'm going to drag you toward the guard, I'll have my back to him so he'll not see my face. He'll come to investigate, when he does you trip him and I'll hit him."

Even in the faint light, Donland saw Dobbs grin, "Aye," he said.

Donland pulled Dobbs by the arms from the corner of the house, the guard called to him in Spanish, "Jose, what you got?" Donland understood and rather than answer, just groaned.

The guard left his post and came to within inches of Donland to stare down at Dobbs. When he did, Donland jerked the pistol from his belt and hit the guard hard with the butt. The man staggered but did not go down. Donland hit him again.

"Help me," Donland said as he reached down and gripped one of the guard's legs. Together, they dragged the guard around the corner and out of sight. "Put on his coat and hat and take his place, if anyone comes they'll see you and think it is him," Donland explained.

Chapter Eleven

The door was locked. "Key!" Donland said and Dobbs felt in the pockets of the coat and came away with a key.

"Here, sir!" Dobbs said as he handed over the key.

Donland turned the lock; it was dark inside, as the building had no windows. He pulled the small tin of matches from the guard's coat he was wearing and lit one. Even in the dim light he was able to see three men sitting with their backs against the wall. They looked up at him.

"I'm Lieutenant Donland, I've a ship waiting, let us be away!" Donland announced,

"Who?" One of the men asked as the other two men began to rise.

"Donland," Donland repeated and added, "We've little time!" He then helped the man to his feet.

"Are you Henri?" Donland asked.

"No I'm Lieutenant Henley captain of the packet *Spartan*, he's Henri and he's Brown, a clergyman."

The man Henley indicated said in accented English, I am Henri, how do you know my name?"

"I was sent to rescue you. There's not time, follow me and be quiet!"

Dobbs was facing the house with a pistol in each hand. "Shall I signal?" he asked.

"No," Donland answered. "Let's get these over the wall! I'll lead you follow after these!"

They set off and rounded the corner. Donland was not concerned with the noise; urgency ruled his mind. They reached the tree near the corner of the wall and Donland said to the first man, "I'll give you a leg up, get over the wall and you'll see some men waiting, tell them to come!"

"What men?" the man asked.

"English! Now up you go!"

The man was light and was up and over the wall. He helped the next two and then finally Dobbs. He then grasped the lower limb of the tree and pulled himself up and climbed from the tree to the wall. Honest and the others were waiting.

"Mister Carstairs you and Honest start these towards Fajardo, wait for me on the road!" Donland ordered.

"Aye," Honest answered and grinned.

"Is it him?" Carstairs asked.

Donland answered, "Aye, I believe so! Question him when you reach the road, I'd not this to be in vain!" He stripped off the guard's coat and hat. "I'll inform the others what we are about."

He calmly strolled past the first guard at the gate. A shout in Spanish of "Alarm! Intruders!" sounded from over the wall. Both guards turned to see what was happening in the courtyard and Donland sprinted past them. The men ignored Donland so he raced on to the corner. David was about to peer around the corner and Donland plowed into him knocking him to the ground. Donland shouted to the closest man, "Help him up! Follow me!" He ran on to the next corner and could hear the sounds of running men behind him.

He slowed when he reached the next corner. Carefully, he peered around the corner but saw no one. Dogs were barking and howling all over the town. Men were stepping from their doorways. The way to the road lay a quarter-mile ahead where the street forked to the left. He chose to cross the narrow street and then darted between two houses and onto the crooked narrow alley that would lead to the road to Fajardo. Once into the alley he slowed, the men soon caught up with him. He turned and faced them, "Weapons at the ready! They'll be on to us!"

There was considerable shouting in the streets. Men living along the alley stepped out to see what the commotion was about and seeing Donland and his men they hurried back inside their homes. False dawn was approaching. He slowed to a jog, dodged a tied dog then aimed his pistol at a man holding a machete. The man ducked back into house and slammed the door.

Ahead, five men ran through the intersection the alley and the street. Donland slowed to a walk. The men had not seen him and the others but they would soon come upon Carstairs and Honest. He knew Honest would be ready for them and easily dispatch them. But there would be more.

Muskets and pistols banged just as Donland stepped into the intersection. He drew his pistol, pausing to allow the others following to reach him. Turning he looked back the way the group of five had come, he didn't see more men advancing but he knew they could be coming along another street.

"Marines to the front," he ordered.

The three marines answered, "Aye," and pushed through the gathered group.

Two more pistol shots signaled that the fight ahead was not over. One of the marines raised his musket and fired. The ball tore into the back of a man's head who was busy re-loading a musket.

They were near enough that Donland called out, "*Hornet!*"

From no more than a hundred feet, Honest answered, "Aye!"

The marine that had fired was to Donland's left. Neither saw the tall heavy-set man leap from the shadows until he was on them, a sword flashed and the marine blocked the blow. The second marine raised his musket and fired. The ball buried itself in the man's chest.

Donland advanced cautiously with his pistol in one hand and his sword in the other.

"That's the lot then?" Honest asked.

"Aye, five was all!"

"Lieutenant Carstairs and the prisoners?" Donland asked.

Honest answered, "Sent them on with Mister Welles, thought it best they come to no harm."

"We best be after them, I'm certain we will be pursued so it is imperative that we go with all haste, You lead and I shall remain in the rear with the three marines."

"Aye," Honest said and was about to start off when Donland grasped his arm. In a hushed tone, Donland said, "I've little trust in Carstairs, we must not let him and the freed men out of our sight!"

"Aye, and I'll have a word with Mister Welles, between the two of us we'll manage them," Honest replied and started off.

"You men there," Donland called to a cluster of five men. I need three pistols."

"Aye, sir," one of the men said and handed Donland a pistol and two others also gave up pistols.

"Marines to me, the rest of you go with Honest!" Donland ordered. He gave each of the marines a pistol.

It was full on daylight now. The jungle was beginning to steam with the new heat. Donland found what he sought within minutes, two large trees grew side by side on one side of the road and on the opposite side was a downed tree. It was perfect for what he intended. "You two there and Corporal Jones there," he ordered them. He stood in the road and in less than three minutes he caught sight of the first rider.

"Riders, each of you take those on your side of the road," He ordered the two marines across from him. "Wait for my command and make your shots count. Don't fire until you are certain of your target!" Donland told them.

The riders came on at a trot. There were four of them.

At what Donland judged to be fifty paces he shouted, "fire!"

The marines, true to their orders took their time and fired individually taking down all four riders. Six others suddenly galloped into view.

"Pistols!" Donland shouted.

The riders reigned their horses before reaching where the bodies lay. They jumped from their saddles and fired off two quick shots. Donland was relieved that the marines waited. "They'll try to get around us!" he shouted. "One watch the front and the other reload muskets while watching your flank!"

A hatted head rose above a bush and quickly ducked. More than a minute past before the man again appeared. Donland and the marines were patient. The jungle seemed deadly quiet.

"They are waiting on more," Corporal Jones who was beside Donland stated.

Donland had not considered that and said, "I fear you are right, we best withdraw."

"Aye," Jones replied and added, "I'll go through the brush if I can."

"Go," Donland said and picked up a small shell from the sand. He tossed it across the road at the other two marines. Both turned in his direction. He motioned for them to withdraw. They both nodded and began backing into the brush.

The man again peeked from his bush. He said something in Spanish to someone near. The other man answered and peeked from behind a tree. The second man began to rise and Donland fired. There was an instant yelp of pain and the man disappeared.

Donland began backing away. He slipped into the brush following Jones' footprints in the sand. Briars and thorns scratched and pricked but managed to catch up to the Jones.

There was movement on the other side of the road. Jones called softly, "Wilson?"

"Aye," came the hushed answer.

Donland ordered, "Down the road, double quick! A hundred yards and wait!"

"Aye," Wilson replied as he rose up.

To Jones he said, "Now you, I'll remain to see if they follow.

"Beg pardon, sir, but I'll not leave you," Jones said firmly.

"Aye, good man," Donland answered and began to count in his head. He would wait no more than two minutes. The time of waiting was spent reloading the pistol. Once done he said to Jones, " Time to go, there'll be more than we can stop if we wait."

"I think they've had enough else they would be on us by now," Jones said.

"Aye, perhaps Morrison was one of them that was killed and the others have no stomach for more fighting," Donland suggested.

Wilson and Martin were waiting. Donland asked, "Any sign of our party?"

"No sir, they've gone," Wilson stated. "Are the bastards coming after us?"

Jones answered, "I think not."

Donland nodded, "Let us catch up to our party. Quick march I think."

"Aye, they can't be far ahead," Jones agreed.

Donland was curious as why there was no pursuit. Even if Morrison were dead, his successor would see the value in regaining the prisoner. Yes, they had been bloodied but if recapturing the prisoners and settling the score were important to at least one of them, they would pursue. The only conclusion he could reach was that Morrison had been killed and those remaining decided to be content with his goods. Without a strong leader, they would have no interest in pursuing for by doing so nothing could be gained. That was the way of it with pirates and he hoped it was true this once.

David paused and said to Carstairs, "We should rest and allow Honest to catch up to us."

"Aye," Carstairs agreed.

Henri, Lieutenant Henley and Brown bent by the stream and began scooping water with their hands and drinking. Carstairs paced like a caged cat. "We best be away," Carstairs said after no more than a minute.

"In a moment," David answered, "These men have been captives for over a month, they haven't our strength."

"They'll have us dead if we linger!" Carstairs hissed.

David stooped to scoop some water. He neither heard the man behind him nor was aware of the coming blow that felled him and left him face down in the stream.

Carstairs turned from David and waved his pistol at the three men, "This is our chance to get away, hurry!"

"Why?" Henri asked.

Carstairs' face was red with anger. "Why, because these men are not your friends, that Donland is a cashiered officer seeking to sell you to the highest bidder. We must stay ahead of him and his thugs else you'll be a captive again."

Henri turned to Henley, "Is it so?"

Henley was cautious, "I'd not know for certain. I think it best if we go, he has the pistol."

Henri nodded in agreement and rose.

Carstairs waved the pistol, "You first Henley."

Brown, the clergyman asked, "What of the boy, you can't leave him like that."

"I can and I will!" Carstairs said.

Brown reached down and pulled David from the steam.

The action angered Carstairs and he drew his sword. "I'll run you through, now go!"

Brown obeyed and followed after Henley.

"Is he dead?" Simon asked.

Honest knelt beside David and felt his chest. "No, he's alive, his head's busted. We best carry him. You men cut some saplings to rig a litter. We'll use his coat and some shirts."

"He can have mine," Simon said and began taking his shirt off.

"Should we wait for Lieutenant Donland," Williamson asked.

Honest considered the question. As much as he wanted to wait he knew what Donland would order. "No, we must catch up to Lieutenant Carstairs. The Captain will not thank us for letting that fellow Henri get away from us. We've come all this way and a lot of men have died, we'd best catch up!"

Donland's words of warning came to Honest's mind. He had not trusted Carstairs and there must have been just cause. He'd thought him a coward and a bully and now perhaps a traitor. Officer or no, he'd have the truth from him about how David came to have his head bashed.

"Simon, and you four manage the litter. We've only a couple more miles to go before we reach the town. When you tire, switch off to a mate! The rest of us are going to catch up to Lieutenant Carstairs, he can't be far ahead and with those men as weak as they are, he'll not be able to travel very fast."

"Aye," Simon answered his father.

"Let us be at it!" Honest said and started off at a jog.

Chapter Twelve

The night before, Scott and O'Rouke had returned with only one man. A good seaman so he seemed, but one man was not enough. "Scott you and I are going back into the town this morning. I need at least three more men, even temporarily, if we are to sail from here," Jackson said.

"I tried, but there wasn't a man to be had. I told you that fellow Benson followed us around town and told tales about you to every man that showed interest," Scott said.

"Aye, you told me but I've words for bloody Benson. If he interferes again I'll have his guts for garters and that's no err!" Jackson fumed.

"O'Rouke you mind *Folly*! We'll be back before dark with men. Allow no one aboard!" Jackson said as he went over the side.

"Aye," O'Rouke answered.

The rowing taxed Jackson's strength but there was no other way. Someone had to stay aboard with the new man and Benson would have to be dealt with. And, he would be dealt with, either with pistol, sword or knife. If the bastard interfered, he would be dead.

Thankfully, the sea was calm and the two of them managed the breakers without difficulty. Jackson and Scott both climbed over the gunnel and pulled the boat onto the sand. Jackson turned toward the *Lady Ash*; there was no boat following. He scanned the beach and did not see a boat he thought belonged to Benson.

"Let us be at it," Jackson said. "We'll go to that cantina first and then on to the saloon."

"Won't do no good," Scott quipped.

Jackson was sweating profusely, the late morning sun was hot and there was very little wind on the beach. They entered the small cantina. His tongue was thick in his mouth and he wanted a drink. He knew they only served a weak beer brewed in a pot in the back of the cantina. It tasted more of papaya than anything did. "Cervesa!" Jackson said to the woman as he sat in a chair and removed his hat.

To Scott he said, "I'm getting old and that is the truth of it. I've some money, a ship but no home. I done told you I need a mate to help me. . ." He was interrupted by the woman with the beer.

Scott sipped the beer while Jackson did the same. He set down the tankard and said, "Aye, you've said as much before."

"What I've not said was that if you and O'Rouke hold true then I'll share my profits with you."

"Partners? Part owners?" Scott asked.

"Aye, of sorts but we've not profit in the current venture and without a crew there'll be none in any venture. We need men and bloody Benson can't stand in our way."

"Aye," Scott agreed.

Jackson took another drink of the beer. He decided that none of the three men in the cantina were seamen. They were locals who fished or farmed. "We'll go to the saloon, perhaps a few have sobered up enough to come drinking."

Scott drank deeply from his tankard while Jackson got to his feet. Dutifully he set down the tankard and rose. "Hope they've better beer in the saloon," he said to Jackson's back.

Jackson did not answer but went out the door and turned toward the saloon. His mind was on his task and on Benson.

Standing just inside the door, Jackson saw Benson sitting at a table with another man. The anger boiled inside.

"Ignore him," Scott said only loud enough for Jackson hear.

"Aye," Jackson answered.

There were two other men sitting at tables, neither appeared to be seamen. Scott said, "Still too early for them to be about. We should come back tonight and perhaps by then another ship will call and we can gain some seasoned men."

Jackson scanned the room again. Benson half turned in his chair. The two made eye contact and Benson grinned.

"Tonight," Scott said and he reached and pulled Jackson by the arm.

Jackson did not protest; it would do no good. He would return to *Folly* and wait for evening. His temper was too hot and he was too weak from the heat. He'd wait for the cool of evening before bracing Benson.

Donland caught up with Corporal Jones and the two other marines. "No one following that I can tell. I don't like it. I would have pursued."

"As you said, sir, that fellow Morrison must have been one of them killed. Else, he'd still be after us," Jones said.

"Aye," let us hope that is the way of things," Donland answered. "How far ahead do you think the others are?"

"Not far," Jones said and added. "No more than five or ten minutes." Then he asked, "How far to the town?"

Donland thought and said, "We just crossed the last stream, so I would say no more than another mile and a half."

Jones took in the estimate and said, "We should catch them before they reach the town. There's these tracks in the sand,"

Jones said. "My guess is four men carrying a litter. See how some of the tracks are deeper than others."

Donland was amazed. "How could you know such a thing?"

Jones answered, "I was born in South Carolina up next to the mountains and my daddy and his daddy lived there all their lives. They learned to read sign from the Cherokees."

"Indians?"

"Aye," Jones answered.

Jones had been right for they caught sight of the back of a man several minutes later.

"Let us run!" Donland said.

They set off and soon came within hailing distance of the man. In front of him were four men carrying a litter. Donland ran past the first man and was shocked to see the man on the litter was David. "What happened to him?" he asked.

"Don't know, sir. When we found him he was lying beside that stream back there. Somehow he got his head stove in. He's not said a word but he's breathing, Williamson said."

Donland called, "David!" but there was no response.

Anger welled up in Donland and he asked, "Where's Jackson and the others?"

"Ahead, when we found Mister Welles he was the only one here. Jackson and the others took out after Mister Carstairs and that Henri fellow. I doubt they be mor'n a hundred yards ahead," Williamson answered.

"Jones you and Wilson with me! We've to catch up to Mister Carstairs!" Donland ordered as he began to run.

Honest slowed to a walk while taking in huge gulps of air. His mind was on Carstairs. He tried to reason if bandits ambushed Carstairs and Henri or if for some reason Carstairs had fought with David and ran. In either case, if was up to him to gain possession of Henri. The man was the reason they were here and to lose him now would be disastrous for Donland.

"Ready lads!" Honest said to the men with him as he prepared to run again.

"Someone's coming," Dobbs said.

Jackson turned placing his hand on the butt of the pistol. He was relieved to see it was Donland and Jones.

Donland was soaked with sweat. His breath came in gulps as he stopped and bent double with his hands on his knees.

After several seconds he asked Jackson, "Where is he?"

"Somewhere ahead! I can't for the life me know why he left Mister Welles or if someone took them prisoner. You said you didn't trust Mister Carstairs, suppose he took him for his own purpose?"

Donland straightened, "Duced if I know, but I know we must catch up to him. How far ahead do you suppose?"

"Maybe in the town by now," Jackson answered.

Carstairs urged his captives on past several huts and a church, he entered the first building he came to, a saloon. He stopped before the door and motioned with the pistol for Henri and the other two to enter in front of him.

Benson watched them enter and asked, "What have you?"

Carstairs answered, "I need a boat to take me to the ship anchored out yonder."

Benson recognized the navy lieutenant's coat for what it was and was curious. "Which ship out there?"

"*Folly!*" Carstairs answered. "Have you a boat?"

"Aye, I've a boat and a ship," Benson answered.

Carstairs couldn't believe his ears. It was turning out better than he had hoped. He'd not have to force *Folly's* master to Antigua. "Your ship?"

"Aye," Benson answered.

"Twenty pounds to take us to Antigua?" Carstairs asked.

"Make it forty and we'll be away on the tide," Benson said with a smile.

"Done!" Carstairs said. "I've no time to dawdle, we are being pursued by bandits and need to be away."

Benson rose from his chair. "You have forty pounds on you?" he asked.

Carstairs answered, "I've not forty pounds but Admiral Pigot will gladly pay and possibly more if you demand it."

"Then let us be away," Benson said as he picked up his hat.

Chapter Thirteen

Donland and Jackson led their party through the town. Carstairs was no where to be seen.

"They must have gone into one of the public houses," Donland said.

"Perhaps but I'd wager he's at the beach hiring a boat to take him out to *Folly*. He'll know you will gut him if you catch him," Jackson said.

Donland did not reply but quickened his pace. "There!" he shouted as he spotted a boat nearing *Lady Ash*. "It has to be him!"

"Aye," Honest replied.

"He's planning to hire her to take him to Antigua," Donland surmised. "We best find a boat and go out to her before her captain accepts whatever Carstairs offers."

"Has he money?" Honest asked.

"Not enough, of that I'm certain. He will promise payment in Antigua."

Even as they hurried down to the beach they saw *Lady Ash's* mainsail unfurled.

"She getting under sail!" Donland said.

They stood helpless and watched as the boat bearing Carstairs bumped along side *Lady Ash*. Donland again scanned the beach for suitable boats, there were none. The only boats on the beach were fishing boats. There were three; all were small and none large enough for all of the men. Four fishermen were stowing their nets at the first two boats.

The men bearing David on the litter were making their way down the beach. Donland made his decision.

"Draw your pistol," Donland said. "We've not time to waste with niceties."

"Aye," Honest replied and drew his pistol.

The men's faces showed horror and fear as Donland and Jackson approached with drawn pistols and the group of men following behind them. They wisely held up their hands while rattling off a string of words in Spanish. Donland understood a smattering of words. He answered them in broken Spanish, "I take boats, chase bad men."

The men cried out in English, "No! No! No!"

Honest pushed past Donland and waved the pistol forcing the men away from the boats. "Empty them," Honest shouted!

Dobbs and the others made quick work of tossing out everything but the oars. Those with Donland did not have to be told to get into the boats. Corporal Jones and Wilson lifted David from the litter and laid him in the stink and fish slime of one of the boats.

"Donland! Donland! Donland" A man shouted from the top of the beach.

Donland turned to see who was calling his name and was surprised to see that it was the clergyman, Brown. Following after him was Lieutenant Henley.

As Brown neared he said, "Carstairs has taken Henri! We couldn't stop him or prevail upon him to wait for you."

"I'm sure you couldn't," Donland said as he turned back to the fishing boat.

"What are we to do, we can't stay here," Brown wailed.

Donland understood, Carstairs left Brown and Henley out of necessity. "No, you can't stay here, you'll go with us!"

Brown looked greatly relieved and asked, "Where are you going?"

"Antigua!" Donland answered.

"To *Folly!*" Donland shouted as he stepped over the gunnel still holding his pistol on the fishermen.

The boats were pushed into the surf and men took up the oars. Donland watched helplessly from the fishing boat as *Lady Ash* got under way. He knew it was Carstairs' intention to reach Antigua and to deliver Henri to Admiral Pigot and claim he was the one who led the rescue and succeeded in freeing Henri. Leaving Brown and Henley behind was necessary for he could not allow them to tell how the rescue was accomplished or his small part in it.

Jackson was shouting orders to Scott and O'Rouke before Donland came over the side. It was clear that he fully intended to be prepared to get under way once Donland and the others had boarded. There wasn't a great deal the two men could do but what could be done; they put their hands to it.

"Dobbs, Corporal Smith and you others man the capstan," Donland shouted as he swung his leg over the gunnel.

"Cast those boats off!" Jackson yelled over *Folly's* side as the last two men began to climb the hull.

"You two!" Donland yelled at Williamson and Honest, "Buntlines and clews, get some men to help!"

Donland turned about and to Jackson, "You've the helm!"

"Aye," Jackson answered.

Lieutenant Henley and Brown were in the process of carrying David to the hatch to take him below. "Belay, Mister Henley. I've need of you!" Donland called.

Henley stopped and faced Donland then turned to speak to Brown. The two men sat the litter on the deck.

"Simon, help Reverend Brown get Mister Welles below," Donland said to the youngster.

"Aye, Captain!" Simon answered and took Henley's place.

As Henley neared Donland asked, "Good to have a deck under your heels again Mister Henley?"

"Aye, sir, aye," Henley answered and smiled broadly. He added, "Thought I'd not have the opportunity again."

"Then would you be so kind as to stand as first?" Donland asked.

"Aye, sir, and with the greatest pleasure!" Henley answered.

Folly's sails began to fill. Donland said as much to himself as he did to Jackson, "We'll tack when we've at least two knots!"

Jackson considered Donland's words and agreed. *Folly's* best speed was close to five knots and that was with a strong wind blowing from aft. She was, as Donland knew from experience, a poor sailor and could not match the speed or agility of *Hornet* nor Benson's *Lady Ash*. The best they could hope for was to arrive in Antigua hours behind *Lady Ash*.

The men responded to Donland's orders without complaint. They, as he, were glad to be free of the land and with a deck under their heels. They took to their tasks with energy and enthusiasm. The sweat and the heat of the land only a memory as they basked in the stiff breeze, the smell of salt and tar.

Donland was pleased that the men took to their tasks and that in less time that he had thought possible, *Folly* had all sails set and filled. He looked out to sea and saw that *Lady Ash* had tacked onto an east by south tack sailing close-hauled. It was possible with her sail rig to hold that course for several hours. *Folly* could match the same course but her speed would be so reduced she would not manage steerage.

He strode from amidships to the helm to stand beside Jackson. The trade wind was to their backs "We'll tack due south," he said almost conversationally.

"He'll know what you are about," Jackson said.

Donland responded, "Aye, he will and take a more southerly tack as well. The more time I can force him to use the more time it avails us.

"You have the makings of a course of action?" Jackson asked.

Donland smiled and answered, "Aye, as long as we can stay within sight of her we have opportunity to avail ourselves to changes in wind. Have you power and chain-shot for those four six-pounders?"

"Aye, but to do any damage we have to get in close, at least a hundred yards," Jackson stated.

"Aye, I mean only to damage her not take her. We haven't men enough for that. What of *Lady Ash's* armament?"

"Three's and no more! I've been aboard her and I doubt Benson has decent powder, he's not a navy man."

Donland smiled at that. "More to our advantage!"

Jackson's face clouded and he said softly, "We've little in the way of stores and water."

"How many days?" Donland asked.

"At half rations, today and perhaps two more."

It was a blow Donland had not expected. He could ask a lot and had asked a lot of these men, how much more they would take on, he didn't know. "Let us hope," he said to Jackson, "that we'll not need more than what we have."

"Aye," Jackson answered with strain in his voice.

"I'll to see to Mister Welles," Donland said and turned away.

David was sitting up. Brown had fashioned a bandage for his head.

"How is it with you, Mister Welles?" Donland asked.

"Hurts like bloody hell!" David answered and added, "Pardon Parson Brown."

Brown said nothing but smiled a wry smile.

Donland asked, "What happened?"

David looked at him and said, "We stopped by the stream to wait and to rest. I bent to get water and someone struck me from behind. I've only just gained my senses."

"Parson Brown did you see?" Donland inquired.

Brown nodded. "I did, it was as the lad said, we stopped and drank. When the lad went to the stream Lieutenant Carstairs hit the lad with the butt of the pistol. He then used it to force us to obey him. Henri and I protested to no avail and I pleaded to go to the lad but Carstairs waved me away with the pistol. I do not know why he turned on us. But, he did tell us that you were out for your own purposes, I frankly do not know who to believe."

"Some, but very little I expect, of what Lieutenant Carstairs told you is true. He was placed in command of the landing party that was to find and rescue you and the others. I was subordinate for my role was to be guide and nothing more. At present, I've no ship to command. But that is beside the point, you recall that it was I who brought you out from Morrison's little jail. And, it was I who led your party away from Luquillo. Now I ask you sir, whose life was always in danger, mine or Lieutenant Carstairs?"

Brown did not hesitate, "You bore the brunt of danger and you were the one that freed us. Other than that, I do not know your intention. You may plan to hold us for ransom, I do not know. As God is my witness, I do not know."

Donland pressed, "But you would declare to any who asked that it was I who freed you and not Lieutenant Carstairs?"

"Yes, that I would state as fact!" Brown said.

Donland realized that he had been pressing the man and stemmed his temper. "Parson Brown all that I ask of you is that when the time comes that you state just what you told me, that it was I who freed you."

"I don't see…"

"Parson Brown it is important for I fear Lieutenant Carstairs intends to claim, before our superiors, that it was he and not me who freed you. It is a small point in your mind but for this lad and for me it means our careers. He will take credit where none is due in order to cover his cowardliness. You saw for yourself his depravity when he hit young Mister Welles without provocation. How he threatened you and the others with his pistol. It is, therefore, my intention to bring charges against him when we reach Antigua and your testimony will be required."

"I think I'm beginning to understand and I do see the why of your persistence. When asked, I shall state the facts and if such are beneficial to you then so be it. I can do no more than that."

Donland asked, "You have no doubt that it was Carstairs who unprovoked; hit this lad in the head with his pistol?"

"Sir, I have said as much, now let this be an end to it!" Brown answered voicing his agitation.

"Very well, I will trouble you no more," Donland said.

David asked, "May I return to my duties?"

Donland smiled and said, "Not as yet, I fear when you stand you will fall over like a one-legged bird."

"That is true," Brown added. "A day or two perhaps of rest will set you to rights."

Folly held her course, as did *Lady Ash* until sunset. The men grumbled upon hearing that they would be receiving only half rations. Donland explained that he could not give what he did not have and that he would hold to the coattails of *Lady Ash* all the way to Antigua.

When Scott asked why, Jackson explained, "A ship was lost, men died just to free one man and that man has been taken. The reward that would be yours is going to go to those aboard *Lady Ash*. Now, lads, you've risked your lives for nothing and that ship was lost and those men died for no good purpose. Your reward has been snatched form you, are you going to allow that to stand?"

"What reward?" O'Rouke asked. "We're not the king's lackeys!"

Donland answered him, "I've a pound per man when we reach Antigua! It isn't much but it is what I can and will manage. Is that reward enough?"

O'Rouke asked, "And what of the prisoner, what is the ransom on his head?"

"That I do not know, what I do know is that he is important enough to those in London that they risked over two hundred men and a frigate to gain him. I promise you a reward, the crown doesn't. I do so because bloody Lieutenant Carstairs has to answer to me for injuring Mister Welles!"

Jackson stepped past Donland; his face was red with anger. "This is my ship and I'll kill any man aboard who hinders this voyage. I've a score to settle with that lot aboard *Lady Ash* and no man is going to stand in my way. We will reach Antigua either as *Lady Ash* does or shortly afterwards, it matters not and when we do there are wrongs to be set to rights. Captain Donland has promised you a reward and I'll stand by it! Do your part and your duty, we ask no more!"

There was no more grumbling but the men weren't happy about their lot either. "We best not find ourselves in the doldrums," Jackson said to Donland when they went below.

"Aye," Donland agreed and joked, "I might have to dice you up like a fish and serve you to them."

Chapter Fourteen

The sun rose and Donland stood with Jackson at the helm. "She's far-reached us by at least another mile," Jackson stated.

"Aye, but she's still within sight. At the end of the day that will not be so," Donland said with a hint of gloom.

At mid-morning, *Lady Ash's* sail dipped below the horizon. The wind also became fitful veering from the northeast and more so from due east.

"Change in the weather coming," Jackson observed.

"Aye," Donland agreed. "Squalls from Africa?" Donland asked.

Jackson scanned the sky. There were wispy horsetails high overhead but not much movement. "I'd say not. Most likely something brewing in the south or perhaps west."

During the first dogwatch the wind died completely. *Folly* wallowed in the troughs. The sun bore down with intensity causing all aboard to crave more water. Every man aboard knew the kegs were dry as bones save one and it contained only a third. In the coming hours they would become desperate.

"How much longer?" Donland inquired of Jackson.

"How much longer will the water last or how much longer will we wallow here?"

Donland managed a smile and asked, "Both?"

"The water, I'd say two cups per man remain. The wind, God only know for I've not a guess."

Donland gazed out to sea. Overhead, rigging rattled with the rolling of the ship. Everything was still and each sound no matter how small was easily heard. The smell of melting tar seemed to grow stronger by the second. Two men bickered below deck and their voices carried up through the gratings. The whole of the ship waited for wind.

An hour passed, then an hour and a half more. Donland was aware of the passing of time for his watch seemed constant in his hand. He knew, just as the men aboard did, that if the wind did not return that their situation would turn grave. A ship without wind and no water to drink was destined to become a ghost ship with a crew of corpses. It was not unheard of just as it was not unheard of that in this expanse of ocean that the wind died for days. There was nothing that could be done; not even the lowering of a boat to drag *Folly* to wind would save them. Despair was creeping into Donland's soul.

"Look there!" Jackson said in Donland's ear.

Donland came from his gloom and looked to where Jackson pointed and said. "I've just seen it."

"Aye," Donland said as he observed the sky and the sea. "A westerly if I'm not mistaken!"

"My thought as well," Jackson said and clapped Donland on the back. "You suspected, did you not?"

Donland grinned and said, "God is sometimes merciful to the poor sailorman."

"Aye, but not often," Jackson said.

They stood at the helm and watched the sky and the sea. At the first small ripple of wind Jackson called, "All hands prepare to make sail!"

"Mister Henley, lively there!" Donland called. "We'll not lose one breath of the wind!"

"Aye," Henley answered and ordered the men sitting in the shade of the sail, "On your feet, this may not be the King's ship but I'll still have your arses at the gratings come morning if you don't!"

The two men sprang up.

"Mind the mains'l!" Henley ordered.

They obeyed and swung up into the shrouds.

The wind came, a great gust that instantly filled the sails.

"Steer due east!" Donland ordered Jackson.

"Sir?" Jackson asked as if he had not heard.

"East, Mister Jackson, we will hold all this wind as long as we can. We will have it an hour or more before *Lady Ash*."

What Donland intended dawned upon Jackson and he answered, "Aye!"

The wind propelled them east a good five miles before the rain reached them. Men turned their faces to the rain as they worked. Donland allowed them several minutes before he ordered, "Casks and buckets! Catch all you can!"

The rain fell in a torrent for better than a quarter of an hour and then began to wane. Then the sun began breaking through the remaining clouds. Gone was the coolness and rain the westerly had brought. Regretfully, were gone the strong winds, which had propelled *Folly*. "Mister Henley collect the water, we've none to waste!" Donland ordered.

"Sir," a voice called to Donland's back, he turned.

David said, "I'm fit for duty."

Donland studied him for a long moment and smiled, "Aye, take charge of the mizzen!"

"Thank you, sir," David answered and smiled. Simon followed along behind David.

Honest came over and said, "Never a more worried boy than that one when David was carried aboard."

"Aye, brothers if ever!" Donland said and turned his attention to the ship.

A loud slap of a sail sounded above Donland. "Wind is dying Mister Jackson, we will tack south by southeast!"

"Aye," Jackson answered.

Donland called to Henley, "Tack south by southeast!

"Aye, sir, South by southeast!" Henley shouted.

"Aye," David answered. And ordered the men at the mizzen to the braces to bear up.

"Tack!" Donland shouted.

"Aye, helm over!" Jackson called.

Men hauled on the braces and the yards began to swing. *Folly* slowly paid off. The topsails caught the wind, and she began to round onto her new course, gathering way as she did so. She met the next roller with her port bow, thrusting boldly into it with a splash of spray.

"Well done Mister Henley!" Donland called when the maneuver was completed.

"Think we will far-reach *Lady Ash*?" Jackson asked.

"We'll know after sunset when we have stars. I can take a reading, it won't be accurate but perhaps it will be enough. We were fortunate to run as far east as we did, it may put us in position to at least arrive within an hour of *Lady Ash*."

Henley sat at the table with Jackson and Donland waiting for the hard biscuit to soften in the cup of water. He asked, "Will her captain not have done as we did and tacked east with the gale?"

"He would if he were not so pig-headed stupid," Jackson said of Benson. "He believes his ship is more than capable to out-pace us and we've no way to catch up to him. He would have held course and when the westerly, if it had reached him, came he would have smiled to himself and enjoyed the breeze and added speed. No, he'd not altered course."

Henley, although an experienced sailor did not understand the significance of what Donland had chosen to do. "So, by altering course we've not gained on *Lady Ash*, we merely were able to gather water? What I mean to ask is, if our destination is still the same then will we not arrive well after her?"

Donland smiled and answered, "Our speed eastward was near to six knots with the wind up our skirts, it was all that we could manage. By my estimate we held that for just over an hour before it began to wane, and when it finally died we were well east of *Lady Ash*. Our course is now south by southwest a mere three points. But our speed is greater by about a knot than previous when we were following *Lady Ash*'s course. So, not only have we gained distance to the east toward our destination but we have also gained speed to our destination. *Lady Ash* gained distance but at the cost of speed. When the sun rises I fully expect to be within sight of her once again."

Henley pulled his biscuit from the cup and looked a bit bewildered.

Donland was on deck before sunrise. He waited until the sun was on the verge of coming over the horizon before he climbed the mast with a glass in hand. The sea before him was empty, to the east was a distant island. Disappointment crept into his soul. He had taken a gamble that was proving to be fruitless. The wind was steady and showed no sign of strengthening, he blew a long breath. Just as he began the climb down when he noticed something westward at the horizon. He pulled the glass up to his eye. What he saw and what he knew must be true was *Lady Ash*. He hurried down the shrouds.

"She is west of us!" Donland stated as his feet hit the deck. "That westerly either forced her off course or something happened aboard. No matter, I believe we will arrive in English Harbor just as she does. I would say about midmorning."

"We've all the sail set *Folly* will wear," Jackson said.

"Aye, and with so few men and no cargo it is not possible to add to our progress," Donland stated. "Still, I would prefer to be on the quay before him and relieve him of Henri."

"Aye," Jackson agreed.

Folly continued on with only minor course corrections for the next hour. In that time, *Lady Ash* came nearer.

"Charlestown just there," Jackson said and pointed.

"Aye," Donland answered and lowered the glass from his eye. "*Lady Ash*, has tacked for the run to English Harbor."

Donland continued to watch and what he saw did not make sense. Several minutes passed before he spoke again. "Her tack will intersect our course some miles before we run up to the harbor."

Jackson had also been observing *Lady Ash* and the set of her sail. "Aye. Curious?"

"I will go up," Donland said and reached up to the shrouds. He climbed quickly with the strongest glass tucked in his armpit.

Once on the top'sl yard he steadied himself and used the mast to brace the glass. There was movement on *Lady's Ash's* deck. He watched for several long seconds, focusing and refocusing the glass until his eyes told him what he saw was true. He grasped one of the stays and did something he had not done in years; he slid down the line to the deck. His feet landed with a thud.

"He means to disable us!" Donland said to Jackson. "I saw a nine-pounder on his deck!"

"Gwad! Where in hell did he get that?" Jackson responded.

"Doesn't matter, he'll be firing chain-shot to disable us. He's in range now but he'll not chance a long shot. We've a few minutes. I'm certain Benson was watching me as I was watching him, he will know that I know what he is about."

"Could all be for show," Jackson said.

"Aye, to force us to tack and avoid his shot,"

"*Folly's* sixes will not be in range until it's too late," Jackson added.

Donland considered the situation. If he were to continue on course to the roads, Benson could disable *Folly*, provided he had a gunner capable of training the big gun and firing it. Benson's lack of trust in the gunner would explain his desire to shorten the distance. But, he had Carstairs aboard who was trained in the use of the gun. It was logical then, that since Benson had the gun that he would have powder and shot and Carstairs could train and fire the gun. To hold course would be a gamble.

Donland made up his mind. "Mister Henley, I'll have the port guns loaded and run up, if you please!"

Sir?" Henley answered totally unprepared for the order.

"Now, Mister Henley, the port guns loaded and run up!"

Honest moved before Henley responded. "Dobbs, you heard the captain, move your arse! I'll be gun captain and you load!"

Dobbs did not hesitate nor did the three men Henley ordered to the gun. One of them was the marine, Corporal Jones who stated, "I've always wanted to shoot one of these babies."

"Mister Jackson see to the power and chain-shot, I'll take the helm," Donland said.

"Aye," Jackson replied with a hint of curiosity in his voice. "He'll not beat us to the harbor then!"

"No, and he'll not damage us either," Donland answered.

It took several long minutes for Henley and his crew to prepare and load the first gun. When finished he called, "Gun ready Captain!"

"Aye!" Donland acknowledged. "Three men crews Mister Henley to train and fire, set the other men to the braces, we will tack and take her on the port beam!"

There was a buzz of excitement among *Folly's* small crew as they understood Donland's intentions.

"By Gawd that's brash!" Henley said to Honest.

"Aye, he is that!" Honest replied.

"Gun two ready!" Henley shouted.

"Aye!" Donland answered. "All hands prepare to tack!" Donland shouted and stole a glance at the *Lady Ash*.

"Tack!" Donland shouted and the men began to haul the lines.

Donland fully expected Benson to fire but he did not, instead his sails went round and her rudder sent her scooting away onto a westerly course.

"Belay hauling!" Donland shouted before the sails began to move. "Hold course, brace up!"

He stole a glance at *Lady Ash*; she was still turning.

"Secure the guns Mister Henley, we'll not need them!" Donland ordered.

Jackson came up to Donland, "You called his bluff, did you not?"

"Aye, if I could observe his deck, he could observe mine. Benson had too much to lose and too little to gain, no matter the amount Carstairs promised. A man will not lose his ship for no good purpose."

"Aye, I'd not, not even for you."

Chapter Fifteen

Benson's boat bumped against the quay. Donland was waiting, he was filled with questions but foremost was what had happened to Carstairs.

"Captain Donland," Benson greeted as he stepped onto the quay.

"Captain Benson," Donland responded coolly.

Benson smiled a half-smile. "I regret to tell you that Lieutenant Carstairs had a minor accident as we were coming to port. Seems a block came loose and bashed the young man in the head. He's alive but I fear he'll not be fit for duty."

Donland eyed Carstairs lying in the bottom of the boat. His head was bound in a bandage.

"Not dead you say?" Donland asked.

"No, fortunate man," Benson stated.

"Aye," Donland agreed.

Henri, the tall blond Swede came to Donland and said, "You have rescued me twice it would seem. You are truly a man of great courage. My uncle the Duke of Ångermanland will be most grateful."

Donland took the young man's hand. "Your servant my Lord," he said. "Let us depart and it will be my great pleasure to present you to Admiral Pigot."

Jackson sat down at the table, he had come out of curiosity. Benson sat across from him, his hat on the table and his face

blank but his eyes seemed merry. Jackson did not know what
Benson was playing at but since events had played out as they
had, it would be better to be forewarned. He remembered the
old adage he had learned as a boy, fool me once shame on you,
fool me twice shame on me. No matter what Benson said, he
would be on his guard.

The pints were brought and set before them. "To profit!"
Benson said as he lifted the pint.

Reluctantly Jackson followed suit and responded, "to
profit!"

They drank and Benson set his tankard on the table. He
eyed Jackson, grinned and said, "We should let by-gones be by-
gones. There's no profit in holding grudges. I've just made an
empty passage here, no profit and no prospects. You have done
the same. What do you say we form a partnership of sorts rather
than be competitors, I figure there be more profit in it for both
of us."

Jackson thought to himself, *fool me once, you'll not do it again.*
He answered Benson with a question, "What is your
proposition?"

"As I see it, the plantations sell to buyers who then sell or
contract with either you or me or some other captains. Only
problem with that arrangement is they expect one of us to lower
our charges so as to beat the other man out. I'm thinking, what
if when the cargo is offered that the other doesn't get involved.
So the buyer has to pay the higher charge and then we can split
that overage. That way we both make money even if we don't
carry the cargo."

"Aye, I see your reasoning. But who will keep the record?"

"Surely, you can trust me for I would surely trust you,"
Benson said.

Jackson picked up the pint and drained the tankard. He set
it down and said, "It's empty, I drank it and it was my doing.
Best if you mind what's yours and I mind what's mine." He rose
and walked away from the table. "Fool me once, you'll not fool
me twice," he said to himself as he went to the door. He then

turned his thoughts to how he was going to find Owens and what he would plan for the man when they met. He'd not forgotten and would not forget.

Captain Hood was to receive Donland and Henri in his cabin. Donland was uncomfortable, his uniform was shabby and dirty and he had no hat. All his possessions had been lost when *Brune* exploded.

The marine sentry snapped to attention as Donland and Henri approached the cabin door. The disgust on the marine's face was plain and Donland knew Hood's face would reveal the same sentiment. It could not be helped.

"Lord Ångermanland, your servant," Hood said as they entered.

"Captain Hood, it is a pleasure to meet you," Henri said and then to Donland's surprise he said, "You are most fortunate to have such a suburb and courageous officer under your command such as Captain Donland. I am pleased that you chose him from among your many fine officers to gain my freedom. His reward will surely include a promotion for having preformed above his duty in such hazardous circumstances."

Hood smiled and cast a glance at Donland and said to Henri, "Aye, a fine and courageous officer. I can assure you he will be well rewarded for his sacrifice. May I offer you refreshments?"

"That is very kind of you Captain Hood, very kind, indeed."

Hood indicated a chair for Henri and said to Donland, "Lieutenant Donland, Lieutenant Watley will see to your needs and provide you with what you need to prepare your report."

Before Donland could answer, Henri said, "I will anxiously await hearing of Captain Donland's promotion for his extraordinary service. He more than deserves the title and position of captain!"

"By your leave sir," Donland managed and turned for the door.

Lieutenant Watley was waiting just outside the cabin door. He grinned as the marine guard closed the door behind Donland. "You best get a bath and shave, I'll see to a decent uniform for you. If I don't miss my guess, you'll be sent for to dine with Captain Hood if not Admiral Pigot. Lord Ångermanland seems quite taken with you."

Donland's curiosity got the better of him and he asked, "Who exactly is Lord Ångermanland?"

Watley leaned to Donland's ear and whispered, "the queen's favorite nephew." He added, "You'll get your reward just as Henri promised. There'll be those who will hate your for it."

Of that Donland had no doubt but as Watley showed him to a small cabin, he could not restrain the laugh.

"What do you find humorous?" Watley asked.

"From a commander with a deck under my heels to a captain on the beach with half-pay, a just reward."

Watley drew the curtain. "This is my meager cabin, a good berth and I'll not complain. Have you heard of the Frenchman, Napoleon?"

"Aye," Donland answered as he unbuckled his sword and removed his shirt.

Watley grinned and the grin faded as he saw the many scars on Donland's arms and chest. He asked, "How were you wounded?"

"Which time?" Donland asked while aware that Watley was staring. "Each one was different and each is a story unto itself."

"My word!" Watley exclaimed.

"Mister Watley, you asked if I had heard of Napoleon."

Watley remembered what he was going to say before Donland removed his shirt and answered, "Admiral Pigot stated that a war with France is certain for Napoleon will become emperor of France. The fools in the Admiralty will rue the day when they rid themselves of so many ships and fighting officers. Napoleon will know our weakness and seek to conquer."

"Aye," Donland agreed. "But what is that to me?"

Watley sighed heavily. "Let me explain it this way, a half-pay junior captain on the beach will be in great demand and one, as Henri said, of great courage, even more so. Bide your time for your day will come."

Donland was indeed invited to dine with Admiral Pigot and Lord Ångermanland. When Ångermanland again brought up Donland's reward, Donland was surprised to hear the Admiral say, "I have composed orders for Commander Donland, he will receive them tomorrow and will take up his command the following day."

The word, *command*, reverberated in Donland's brain, he'd not dared to hope for another. *Hornet* was his past, what ship now lay in his future?

Printed in Great Britain
by Amazon

80978357R00079